Keeping Holiday

Keeping Holiday

Starr Meade

CROSSWAY BOOKS

WHEATON, ILLINOIS

Keeping Holiday
Copyright © 2008 Starr Meade

Published by Crossway Books
        a publishing ministry of Good News Publishers
        1300 Crescent Street
        Wheaton, Illinois 60187

Design and typesetting by Lakeside Design Plus
Cover design and illustrations by Justin Gerard, Portland Studios
First printing 2008
Printed in the United States of America

Trade Paperback ISBN: 978-1-4335-0142-5
PDF ISBN: 978-1-4335-0436-5
Mobipocket ISBN: 978-1-4335-0437-2

Library of Congress Cataloging-in-Publication Data
Meade, Starr, 1956–
     Keeping Holiday / Starr Meade.
        p. cm.
     Summary: Each year Dylan's family visits Holiday, and this time his determination to bring home the feelings and experiences of that special place leads Dylan and his cousin Clare on a journey through such places as the Forest of Life and Winterland as they seek the Founder and the true Holiday.
      ISBN 978-1-4335-0142-5 (tpb)
      [1. Faith—Fiction. 2. Voyages and travels—Fiction. 3. Christian life—Fiction. 4. Allegories.] I. Title.

PZ7.M483Kee 2008
[Fic]—dc22
                                        2008010449

VP   16 15 14 13 12 11 10 09 08
         9   8   7   6   5   4   3   2   1

Contents

Holiday Vacation

he car, already barely moving, came to a complete stop. Dylan looked out his window at the car in the next lane, then at the car on the other side. Neither of them moved either. "Guess we'll be sitting here for a while," Dad said, but he wasn't complaining.

"It's just like last year and the year before that," Mom said, and she wasn't complaining either.

No one ever complained about the traffic jams going into Holiday. Everyone knew they would occur, but no one seemed to mind. Traffic jams anywhere else caused tempers to boil like overheated radiators, but motorists stuck in traffic on the way into Holiday whistled and smiled at one another, waiting patiently for their turn to go.

Dad rolled down his window and stuck his nose out. Closing his eyes, he breathed deeply and smiled. "Ah," he said, "those wonderful Holiday smells. I've been looking forward to this vacation all year."

Everyone looked forward to going to Holiday, at least everyone Dylan knew. The town drew the same devoted visitors year after year. People never grew tired of it. For months in advance, they would busy themselves with elaborate preparations, planning to get the very most out of this year's stay in Holiday. For several weeks now, Dylan's neighbors had all been greeting each other with, "Are you all ready for your trip?" or "Do you have much left to do before you go to Holiday?"

Mom turned to Dylan, winked, and smiled. "Wonder what souvenirs you'll find this year?" she said.

"Whatever they are, I'm sure they'll be fine," Dylan answered.

"Well, that's a switch," Dylan's father said. "I remember when it seemed like the only part of the vacation you cared about was the gift shop!"

"That's because I was little," Dylan replied. "When you're little, you don't appreciate all the other stuff."

"Like . . . ?" Dad prodded.

"Like the food," Dylan said. "And how pretty everything is. And how much fun it is to be with everybody—playing games and singing and laughing. Why can't it be like that at home?"

"Are you sure it can't be?" Mom asked.

"Well, it isn't, anyway," Dylan answered. "And I don't see *why* it isn't. You can eat the same food with the same people and try to do everything just the way it's done in Holiday, but it's never the same."

"I suppose that big pile of last year's souvenirs I saw in the garage marked 'give away' is part of what you mean," Dad said. He chuckled. "And after all the time it took for you to choose those. Good grief! I thought we'd have to spend our entire vacation in that store!"

Dylan felt a touch of embarrassment, but he bravely admitted, "Well, yeah, that's what I mean. The souvenirs always seem so wonderful in the gift shop. But once you get them home, they just become more stuff to sit on the shelf."

"You're not tired of going to Holiday, are you?" Dad asked.

"No," Dylan said. "But I think there's more to it than souvenirs. More to it than food and pretty things and people, too. Because none of those things are ever the same at home. There's something to the town of Holiday that makes things different, better than they are anywhere else. I just don't know what is."

Mom glanced at Dad and said, "Our little boy's growing up."

Dylan scowled to himself and thought, *What's that supposed to mean?* But the thought flew from his mind as a space finally cleared for their car and it inched ahead, through the city gate into Holiday. Dylan sat up, stirred by that same old Holiday excitement, and watched out the window to see what had changed since last year.

"Ah, those wonderful Holiday smells," Dad said again, taking a deep breath. Dylan copied him, and breathed in a great cloud of sharp pine fragrance. Full pine trees and tall, dark green firs lined both sides of the road. *They're like old friends,* Dylan thought to himself, *welcoming us back.* The car moved slowly on, and Dylan caught new fragrances mingling with the scent of pines. He smelled sweet spicy smells and scents of woodland herbs and, over and underneath it all, the pungent odor of wild green plants growing.

As the car inched through the crowded streets, other fragrances floated in the window: meats roasting, breads baking, sweets simmering.

"Oh, look at how pretty it is!" Mom exclaimed. "I didn't think it could possibly be better than last year, but I do believe it is."

Though the streets were full, they were spotlessly clean. Houses wore fresh coats of bright paint, their doors and windows cheerily accented to match. Open shops beckoned. Each store window tried to outdo the last with its inviting display of the wonders to be found inside. Ropes of lights, strung back and forth across the street, twinkled with promises of magic. Glittering decorations climbed up or hung down from every available space.

Visitors thronged the sidewalks and stores. Some wandered into shops, coming back out again with additions to their already huge piles of packages. Others sat with their friends at the many little tables in café windows and on sidewalks, tables loaded with roasted meats, breads, fruits and nuts, and sugary cakes. From somewhere nearby came strains of fiddle music. When Dylan thrust his head out the car window to hear better, a warm glow from an upstairs window caught his eye. Happy dancers whirled in and out of view in the window. A little farther on, a group of happy vacationers walked by on the sidewalk, arm-in-arm and singing at the top of their lungs.

Dad turned the car into a parking lot and pulled into a space. Carrying their bags, Dylan's parents headed toward the entrance underneath the sign that read, "WELCOME TO YOUR HOLIDAY HOME AWAY FROM HOME." Dylan looked at the sign for a moment and thought, *Holiday feels more like home than home does.* Then he picked up his bag and followed his parents.

Dylan swallowed his mouthful of cinnamon bread and washed it down with a gulp of milk. "Why don't we ever have this for breakfast at home? Can't you buy it there?" he asked.

"I could probably order it at the bakery," his mother answered.

Dylan considered. "But I'll bet it wouldn't be the same," he said. "Why *is* that? Why are things we do at home never quite as good as when we do the same things in Holiday?"

Dylan's parents glanced at each other, with the expression that usually made Dylan say, "What?" But just now he was too intent on his question. "Yesterday, for example. That party was so much fun!"

Mom nodded and Dad said, "Wasn't that great?"

"But what did we do?" Dylan continued. "Nothing we couldn't do at home. We played games, we sang songs, we ate. We hardly ever play games at home and when we do, they're boring. And no one ever sings. Plus, all the people at the party are people we could get together with back at home. But we never do. And if we did, I'll bet we wouldn't really get along very well. Why does Holiday make everything we do so different?" A sudden idea occurred to Dylan, causing him to set down his milk glass so hard that some of the milk splashed out. "Hey! Have you ever thought of moving to Holiday to live?"

"Holiday's a vacation town," Dad replied. He poured himself another cup of coffee. "Everyone's here on vacation. There'd be no job for me if we lived here."

Mom passed Dad the sugar and said to Dylan, "You'll just have to look for a way that you can *keep* Holiday, even when we go home." She glanced at her watch. "Done with your breakfast, Dylan? Better run off and get ready. We need to leave for church in five minutes."

At the church, a middle-aged man, already sitting in the pew Dylan's family selected, smiled at them. "Hi, there," he said, nodding cheerfully. "My name's Mr. Smith," and he shook hands with Dylan and his parents. Mr. Smith's chubby face beamed as he said, "I just love going to church in Holiday, don't you? I never go at home, but I wouldn't dream of skipping church in Holiday." The music began then, cutting off the pleasant little man's comments. He didn't seem to mind. He opened his songbook with a flourish and nodded his balding head to the beat. He sang loudly, and though he took an occasional peek at the page through his glasses, he seemed to have these particular songs memorized.

Dylan sang too, but he looked around as he sang. The old stone building was full. This was odd enough, since Dylan was used to seeing churches at home half empty. But even more than that, almost everyone in the church was singing with enthusiasm. Not many people sang at home. Dylan himself would prefer not to sing in church, but his parents always insisted. In fact, the comments of his neighbor in the pew made complete sense to Dylan. Like him, Dylan would probably skip church at home too, if his parents did not require him to go. And yet, just as the pleasant-faced man had said, he wouldn't dream of missing church in Holiday. He even felt perfectly content to sing. Dylan puzzled over what the difference could be. Church in Holiday was just *more*. More what? Dylan asked himself. More full somehow. There seemed to be more *behind* it all. Church here was more joyful too and, at the same time, more serious. Dylan shook his head to clear it of all these busy thoughts and turned his attention to the candles being lit up front.

When the service ended, the man in the pew gave a deep sigh. Then he stood up. "Well, that's done till next vacation. It *was* lovely, wasn't it? Nice sitting by you," he said to Dylan's family and walked away.

"Is it okay if I walk back?" Dylan asked his mom. The little Holiday church sat on the very end of the street, with the forest coming right up against it. Dylan wanted to take his time, walking back down the street to their hotel, savoring the Holiday sights and sounds one last time.

"I don't see why not," she answered. "Just don't be late for lunch. You wouldn't want to miss our last big Holiday get-together. You know we go home tomorrow."

Dylan made a face. "Don't remind me," he said. Slipping out a side door in the church to avoid the crowd, Dylan found himself in a quiet little garden he had never seen before. The winding brick path led to a gate in the little fence. Even from a distance, Dylan could see something bright red leaning against the fence, as though it had been propped up there on purpose. As he drew nearer however, he saw that it was only a piece of paper with some lettering on it—an advertisement for something. He bent to pick it up, then stared at it, startled. It read:

"Would you like to KEEP Holiday?"

That was what Dylan's mom had said at breakfast: "You'll just have to look for a way that you can *keep* Holiday, even when we go home." He had wondered what she meant when she had said it, but then they had hurried off to church, and he had forgotten about it. Besides, Mom was always saying things like that, things that made you wonder what in the

world she was talking about. Dylan read the rest of the flyer. It contained only these few words: "Pass through the church garden gate for more." The path that led from the gate was immediately swallowed up by the thick woods that came right up to the garden fence.

Dylan felt that he must at least start down the path, to see if he could find out what the red paper meant. He would hurry, just for five minutes, then make it up by running back to the hotel.

As it turned out, it took Dylan only three minutes of winding through trees and around corners to learn what he needed to know. The road emerged from a particularly thick stand of trees into a clearing, then turned abruptly to avoid going over the edge of a precipice. Dylan stepped out to the edge and looked down into a valley. Nestled in this valley was a town. Dylan had never seen a town like this one before. Every building had its own unique and beautiful appearance, as though a school of architects had held a contest here to see who could design the most wonderful building. The whole town was surrounded by a high wall, which glistened in the sunlight with bright gleams of first one color, then another. The city was not so far below that Dylan could not hear sounds floating up from it. He held his breath to listen and caught traces of music unlike any he had ever heard, so beautiful that he immediately decided he had never really heard music until that moment. Every now and then, a fragrance wafted up to him from below as well, a fragrance so delicious that he closed his eyes and breathed in as deeply as he could.

"What *is* this?" he whispered to himself, looking around for some clue to the astonishing city. Then he saw the signs. "Vista Point," the small one by the side of the path read. The second line of the same sign said, "City of Holiday." Another sign stretched from tree to tree over the top of the path, which continued along the edge of the precipice, evidently to a way down into the valley. This sign said, "Entrance to Holiday straight ahead."

If that's Holiday down there, Dylan thought, *where have we been all this time?* He stepped under the sign and turned around to see what it said on the other side. To his amazement, he read the words, "Holiday Visitors' Center" and saw an arrow pointing back the way he had come. He looked back down into the valley at what was, evidently, the *real* Holiday. The streets of this town held sights and sounds and smells that made the old Holiday, the one Dylan had always loved, seem like just a little model of something. *Visitors' center?* Dylan thought. *We've spent every vacation of my life in Holiday and we've*

never gotten past the Visitors' Center? Well, it was time to remedy that now!

Intent on seeing the "more" promised by the flyer, Dylan hurried off down the path. From somewhere very close, a motor whirred. A long wooden barricade slammed down in front of Dylan. Only then did he notice the little guard booth with the man inside. "Sorry," the man said to Dylan, "authorized personnel only."

"Well, then what does this mean?" Dylan asked him, polite but insistent. He held up the flyer. "It seems to be an advertisement of some kind, and it tells people that they can see more of Holiday. Why does it say that if people can't really go down there and get in?"

The guard examined the bright red flyer. A minute went by in silence. Then the guard said, "It doesn't say if they want to *see* more; it just says 'for more.'"

Dylan did not see how that made any difference. "Okay, but still," he said, "how can that be if people can't get in?"

The guard examined the flyer for another silent minute. "And," he pointed out, "it doesn't say 'if you want to *see* more of Holiday'; it asks if you want to '*keep* Holiday.'"

Dylan sighed. "But the point is," he said, "that it tells people to go through the church garden gate, but you're saying they can't get into Holiday."

"I'm not saying people can't get into Holiday," the guard protested. "I'm saying only *authorized* people can get in. I don't make the rules," he added, "I just help keep them."

"Well, then, how are people authorized to get in?" Dylan asked. "Can I get authorized? I'd really like to see more—I mean, I'd really like more," he corrected himself. "And I've been wondering how to keep Holiday. Who authorizes people to go in?"

"The Founder does," the guard answered helpfully. "And I can't think of any reason why he wouldn't authorize you, when he's authorized so many others."

"Okay," Dylan said, encouraged. "Where do I find the Founder?"

"Oh, you can't find the Founder; he finds you," the guard replied. "He's not just the Founder; he's the finder too!" He chuckled. "That rhymed!" Then he grew serious. "But until he finds you, I'll have to ask you to go back the way you came. You can't go in."

Dylan's shoulders slumped with disappointment. He turned away from the barricade and looked back down over the edge, at streets that glittered with the promise of wonders he had never known. He closed his eyes to better smell the scents that the breeze carried up. They were scents that could go to your head and make you forget everything, yet they were delicate enough to make you long for more. As he stood there, eyes closed, breathing in the wonderful fragrances, the music swelled from below so he could hear every note distinctly. It played just for him; he was sure of it. He *must* go where it called—but instead, he had to turn away and head back to his family's lodging, the little hotel that was only a part of the Visitors' Center.

2

Finding Where to Start

*J*ust as Dylan had expected, Clare said nothing when he finished telling her his story. She certainly did not say (as several had), "Are you sure you weren't imagining things? Or maybe you dreamed it." Nor did she say (as most did), "Hmm. Interesting. Wanna go play ball?" She said nothing. She sat on the step of Dylan's front porch, thinking about what she had heard. Dylan could tell she was thinking by the faraway look in her brown eyes and by the absentminded way she twirled a lock of her sandy blonde hair around and around with her fingers.

When Dylan had first returned from the vacation during which he had found a greater Holiday *beyond* Holiday, he had tried to tell people about it. For the most part, no one cared. His parents had listened to his story attentively and certainly acted as if they believed him. But they had exchanged those glances with each other that drove Dylan crazy. They had not said much about his discovery. No one else had seemed at all interested. So Dylan had said no more about it, although he had never stopped wondering.

Today, however, Clare had said, "Too bad for my parents that they have to be gone at Holiday time! But I'm going to have fun, going with you guys instead. Aren't you excited about Holiday, Dylan?" Even as she was asking the question, the thought had flashed through Dylan's mind, *Clare! I can tell Clare. She'll understand.* Dylan had always preferred Clare to all his other cousins. There was more to her. *She's different from other people,* Dylan had said to himself, *more thought-y.* So Dylan had told Clare the whole story.

Now Clare finally spoke. "What happened when you went back?" she asked. Just like Clare! Everyone else, when they said anything at all, said, "Did you ever go back?" Clare *knew* Dylan would have gone back to look at the bigger Holiday again. It was what she would have done herself.

"We've been back on vacation three times since then," Dylan answered. "And each year, I've gone to that church every day, and out into that garden—but the weird thing is, there's never been a gate in the garden fence. And it's not just that someone has reworked the fence—the path that led on, away from the gate, isn't there either. Just woods and nothing more. But I know I went through a gate and down a path. And the gate's on the flyer."

Clare's face lit up. "You still have the flyer? Could I see it?" She scooted over on the step so Dylan could get past her and in his front door. In a moment, he returned with the red flyer, now worn with repeated folding and unfolding. Clare took it and read it. Sure enough, there it was.

"Would you like to KEEP Holiday? Pass through the Church Garden Gate for More."

Clare's eyes glowed. "How exciting—a real mystery! Trying to solve this will make going to Holiday even better than ever."

"Well, yes and no," Dylan answered, although he did feel better already, now that he had someone who would help him try to solve the puzzle Holiday presented. "It's much more than just a mystery. It's much more than just wanting to know what happened to that door. You know how we've always loved Holiday—everyone loves Holiday." Clare nodded. "But the Holiday we've always known is *nothing* compared to the other one I found. I could tell that just by standing there, even though I didn't get to go in. And now I want to get into the real Holiday so much that I'm not very interested in the old one anymore."

Clare nodded. She could see how that would be. "It must be kind of like the difference between a picture of something and the real thing—like this orange," she added, holding up the one she had just finished peeling. "Somebody could be a great painter, but he can only paint what an orange *looks* like. It's just a picture. You can't smell it or taste it or feel the bumps on the peeling, because it's not a real orange." She paused, then added, "And I guess that if you're really hungry for an orange, looking at a picture of one just makes it worse."

"That's exactly how it feels," Dylan said, and once again, he was pleased with how well Clare always understood things.

"It seems to me," Clare continued, "that what we really need to do is figure out some way to find the Founder—whoever he is. He could authorize us to get in *and* tell us where the entrance is."

"But that's just it," Dylan pointed out. "That guard told me you *can't* find the Founder. So if I can't find the Founder *and* I can't find that door again—it seems hopeless!"

"What about the requirements for being authorized?" Clare asked. "Do you know what they are? What kinds of people get authorized?"

Dylan shook his head. "I have no idea," he said. "I'm a little worried about that—maybe I won't meet the requirements. But I really want to get into Holiday, more than I want anything in the world. So whatever it takes to *get* authorized, I think I'd do it. Anyway," he concluded, "two heads are better than one. Maybe with both of us working on it this year, we'll figure something out. I'm glad I told you. And I'm glad you're going with us."

Traffic jams being worse than ever, it was quite late by the time the family car pulled into the hotel parking lot in Holiday. Clare, Dylan, and his parents got nothing done before bedtime except for unloading the car and partially unpacking their bags. Their first stretch of free time in the morning found Dylan and Clare entering the front door of the old stone church, empty in the middle of a weekday.

They went straight to the garden to examine the fence. They went all the way around it twice, looking very carefully and even feeling every inch with their hands to be sure. With their careful searching finished and with nothing to show for it, Dylan and Clare stepped back inside the building and dropped into a pew. "Now what?" Dylan wondered out loud.

"Look, over by the front door," Clare pointed. "An information rack. Maybe it tells something about the church or shows a map of it or something. Let's go see." They hurried over and looked through the few different papers in the rack. They found a schedule of services, a list of telephone numbers for the minister and for others who worked with the church, and an advertisement for a book. They did not find any information about the church building or its layout, nor did they find anything that mentioned a garden gate or a real town of Holiday.

"How frustrating!" Clare complained.

"It's always like this," Dylan said. "I know there's more to Holiday than what we see. I know what the flyer says. I know what I've seen. But I can never get anywhere at trying to find out more!" He shook his head. "And the more I can't get into Holiday, the more I feel like I just *have* to!" He sighed. "Anyway, for now, we're supposed to join Mom and Dad for a shopping trip. We'd better get going."

Back at the hotel, Mom and Dad said they would be ready soon. Dylan and Clare went to their rooms to change clothes. A little later, as they walked out the door of the hotel and headed for the first store, Clare whispered to Dylan, "I found something in my room I've got to show you later."

Dylan enjoyed shopping with Clare and his parents. No one could have a bad time shopping in Holiday. The best of moods always prevailed in the stores. No one ever seemed impatient or cross. And the shopkeepers, as always, had done such a good job of making their stores attractive—almost as though they meant to entertain guests rather than sell merchandise. Nonetheless, Dylan could not shake off the certainty that there was something else—something bigger and much more important than buying things—just under the surface waiting for him to discover it. He felt sure that whatever Clare had found in her hotel room had something to do with it.

When they finished their shopping, it was time for lunch. Then the dishes needed to be washed and put away. Finally, Mom went to lie down for a short nap, and Dad settled back with a newspaper. Dylan turned to Clare. "So what did you find?" he asked.

"I'll go get it," she answered and ran upstairs. She came right back carrying a hardbound black book. There were no pictures on the front or anything to make the book appear at all interesting.

"A book," Dylan said. "Doesn't look like much to me."

"No, it doesn't look like much," Clare agreed. "But don't you recognize it?"

Dylan looked again. "We saw an advertisement for that book somewhere," he said. "In one of the stores, I guess."

"No," Clare said, "we saw the ad in the information rack at the church. That's why, when I found the book in the back of one of my dresser drawers, I wanted to see what it was." She turned the book so that she could read the title on the side. "*A Guide to Holiday for Visitors and Residents,*" she read. "That sounded like it might be helpful, so I started flipping through the pages. I couldn't understand most of it. There were a lot of rules and explanations of things and some history stuff. I'd just about decided it wouldn't help us when I turned to the very front and found this." Clare handed the black book to Dylan, with the page opened to the section she meant. Dylan took it and read.

"The Holiday we see today is very old, having existed for centuries. It was, however, originally built upon the ruins of a city even older. Cruel and powerful tyrants ruled the ancient city. When a strong, kind king rescued the townspeople by over-throwing the evil tyrants, the joyous citizens wanted to raise a monument to honor their liberator and his overwhelming victory. What better monument could they erect, they thought, than to transform the city, built to honor tyrants and enslave multitudes, into a world-renowned center of beauty and joy in honor of their savior? The people had to tear down much of the old city, but they used what they could to build the new one. Thus Holiday was established and quickly became the favorite resort of millions. Every year, in all the centuries since its founding, people have flocked from all over the world to visit Holiday.

"Most visitors to Holiday, however, never get any farther than the Visitors' Center. Official authorization is required to enter the real city of Holiday, authorization that only the Founder can grant. Persons who hold this official authorization may come and go in Holiday at all times. Persons who would like more of Holiday but who have not received authorization may find a temporary visitor's permit helpful. Visitors' permits are available in the information rack of the church located in the Holiday Visitors' Center."

"But we looked in the information rack in the church," Dylan protested, when he had finished reading. "There were no visitors' permits. We would have seen them."

"We'll just have to look again," Clare answered. "We're going to church for a service tonight. We'll look then."

Dylan and his family slipped into a pew in the crowded church just as the choir began to sing. In front of them, a man whose hair was going gray and getting thin, especially in the center, turned to welcome them. He grinned and waved a small, discrete wave. Then, pushing his glasses back up on his nose, he turned back around. Dylan leaned over and whispered to Clare, "No matter where we sit, we always end up sitting by that guy! His name's Mr. Smith."

As soon as the service was over, Dylan and Clare left Dylan's parents talking with the man in the pew in front of them while they headed back to the information rack. "Look! I'll bet those are the visitor's passes!" Clare pointed at a stack of bright green cards in the rack.

"That's really strange!" Dylan said. "You saw—they weren't there yesterday!" Clare took a green card from the rack. Sure enough, across the top in large letters were the words, "Visitor's Pass."

Dylan took one too. He turned his over and saw a list in fine print, under the words, "Terms of Use." He began to read out loud.

"This pass entitles the bearer to enter Holiday, on a temporary basis only, without securing official authorization.

"This pass is good for four days from the bearer's first entrance into Holiday. It expires at sundown of the fourth day.

"This pass is non-renewable.

"Keep this pass on your person at all times and be ready to present it when called upon to do so at any time during your visit in Holiday.

"Failure to present this pass when asked to do so will result in

(1) a costly fine;

(2) immediate expulsion from Holiday;

(3) and the forfeiture of all right to ever return."

Beside them, someone chuckled pleasantly. Startled, Dylan and Clare looked up to see Mr. Smith. He looked over Clare's shoulder at the pass she held. "Reading the rules for visiting Holiday, are you?" he asked, good-naturedly. "Did you get those passes in the children's class?"

"We didn't go to a children's class," Clare answered. "We got them from right here in this rack," and she pointed to the stack of green cards.

"Well, what do you know," Mr. Smith replied. "You usually only find those being given out in children's classes."

Dylan turned the visitor's pass over in his hand. Nothing on it said that it was for children only. "Can't grown-ups have these?" he asked.

"Oh, it's not that they *can't* have them," the man said. "But what would they do with them now that they're grown up? The passes say they're for going into the *real* Holiday, right?" Dylan and Clare nodded. Mr. Smith nodded too. "Right. Back when we were little, we all believed in a bigger and better Holiday that would last all year. But . . . " and he shrugged and made a sad face, "too bad for us, we grew up."

"But there *is* a bigger and better Holiday," Clare protested. "Dylan's seen it."

The man chuckled again and patted Dylan on the head with a soft, white hand. "Of course he has," he said. "You children have a good evening. And don't grow up too fast." And Mr. Smith moved away and out of the church door.

"Is it just me?" Clare asked. "Or is that guy a little strange?"

Dylan waved his hand, as if to brush away her concern. "He's okay. You know how grown-ups can be sometimes. I'm sure he means well. But Clare, look at this!" And Dylan pointed to a line on the front of the green pass. He read it out loud. "To find the visitors' entrance into Holiday, exit from the gate in the church garden." Dylan looked up. "You see! That's what I remember! There *was* a gate in the garden—I first found the red flyer leaning against it. But I've been back to the garden many times since. The gate's never been there. I've never again seen anything that looked like any kind of entrance into anywhere."

"Well, we'll just have to come check it out tomorrow," Clare said. "It's too dark now. And your parents are ready to leave. Let's go."

Dylan's parents had planned a shopping day "for adults only," as they said. Dylan and Clare understood that to mean that at least part of the shopping would include surprises for them. As his parents prepared to go, Dylan showed them the green visitor's passes he and Clare had picked up. His mother examined one carefully, then handed it to Dylan's father with a smile. "At last," she said softly. "Of course, it's all right if he goes?"

Dylan's father nodded and handed the pass back to Dylan. "This may be the most important trip you'll ever make," he told Dylan, surprising him with his serious tone. "Keep your eyes and ears open, and pay attention to everything. If you need to be gone the whole four days that the pass allows, do it. You'll never do anything as important as getting authorized to keep holiday."

Dylan could not believe what he was hearing. "You sound like you've been there," he said. "Have you?"

Not just his father but Dylan's mother also nodded solemnly. "Of course we have, and our dearest wish is for you be authorized to go as well," his mother told him.

"Why haven't you ever taken me?" Dylan wanted to know.

"We've taken you as close as we can," she answered. "The rest of it is a trip you must make on your own. Like your father says, pay careful attention, and make every effort to find the Founder."

Dylan shook his head. "No, you can't find the Founder," he said. "I've already been told that."

"But he has a way of being found, nonetheless," his mother answered. That was all she would say, except for urging Dylan and Clare to be careful and to be sure to take water with them, as well as some fruit and sandwiches. As she kissed him goodbye before going out the door with her husband to do her shopping, Dylan thought her eyes looked a little teary.

In a matter of minutes, the cousins had packed a few sandwiches and grabbed a few apples. Then they hurried to the church and through the front door (doors were never locked in Holiday). Dylan was heading single-mindedly for the door to the garden when Clare stopped him by calling, "Dylan! Look!" He stopped and looked where she pointed at the information rack. "It's empty again. Just like it was when we were here the other day. That whole stack of visitor's passes is gone."

Dylan saw that she was right. There was no sign of the green passes. "Maybe that man came back and got one after all," he said.

"Right," Clare laughed. "And took them all to hand them out to his grown-up friends!" She stopped laughing and be-

came thoughtful. "Maybe the passes are only available when the church is open for services."

Dylan was already moving ahead again. "Maybe," he answered. "Come on." And he opened the door to the small, enclosed garden. There was the gate, just as he remembered it. Today, however, the garden was not empty. A man sat on a folding chair next to the gate. Dylan thought he recognized the same man who had guarded the entrance to Holiday when Dylan had seen it three years ago.

The man did not seem to recognize Dylan, however. "Good morning," the man said. "Got your passes?"

"Right here," Dylan nodded eagerly, holding up the pass. Was he actually going to get into the real Holiday at last?

"Now, you do understand, don't you," the man said, "that you must keep these passes with you at all times?" Both Dylan and Clare nodded. "Lose 'em," the man continued, "and you lose the right to be in there at all—ever—*and* you'll get stuck with a hefty fine. And you also understand that once you go in you have a total of four days for using this pass, then it expires for good. After that, you can only get in again if you've been authorized. And only the Founder can authorize you."

"Yes, we know," Clare answered for both of them. "Do you think we'll find the Founder once we get into Holiday?"

The little man peered at Clare, as though she had said something truly startling. After a minute of staring, he answered, "You don't find the Founder; he finds you." He paused briefly, and added, "He's not just the Founder; he's the Finder, too." He paused again. Then his face broke into a grin, and he opened his mouth to say one more thing.

But before he could say it, Dylan said quickly, "That rhymed." The man's mouth snapped shut and the grin disappeared. "It *did* rhyme," he said quietly. Then, he stood and inspected both of their passes. "Have a nice visit," he said, and held open the gate that led from the garden.

3

No Way Out

Dylan stepped through the gate first, with Clare right behind him. They hurried down the path to the overlook, and looked down. There it lay, the real Holiday, its walls, its towers, and its banners glistening in brilliant shades of red, gold, green, and blue. Clare stood still and stared, her mouth open. She closed it at last, then opened it again to say, "Oh, Dylan, isn't it beautiful?"

Dylan nodded. "I can only imagine what it's like up close! Come on," he said and started off down the path leading to the city. The barricade that had stopped him before was up. He stepped past it, Clare right behind.

Then Clare called, "Dylan, wait." Dylan looked back to see Clare pointing to a sign just on the other side of the road. "Look."

Dylan looked at the wooden, arrow-shaped sign. It pointed in exactly the opposite direction from the entrance to the beautiful city. The words on the sign read, "FIRST-TIME GUESTS TO HOLIDAY. THIS WAY."

"That's crazy!" Dylan said. "Anyone can see that Holiday is the other direction. It's not that way at all. Come on. Let's go the way we can *see* we should go." Dylan turned back and set out once more toward the city. Clare hesitated, shrugged, then followed. She had to hurry to keep up. Dylan, in his excitement, walked briskly, talking all the while.

"It's not just that it *looks* pretty," Dylan said to Clare. "There's so much more to it than just the way it looks. It's the way it smells and the sounds you can hear—and just the way it makes you *feel*. I want to feel that way forever. . . ." Dylan's voice trailed off and he stopped in his tracks, looking at another wooden, arrow-shaped sign they had come to. The sign pointed back the way they had come. "FIRST-TIME VISITOR?" it said, in large letters. In smaller letters underneath were the words, "WRONG WAY."

Dylan looked at the sign suspiciously, as though he suspected it of playing a joke on him, but he said nothing. He shook his head slightly and continued on, without changing direction. The children walked on in silence for a few more minutes until they came to yet another sign, again of wood and in the same shape, pointing back the way they had come. This one read: "WARNING! WRONG WAY FOR FIRST-TIME VISITORS!"

"Maybe we *should* go back the other way," Clare suggested. "What you really want is to get authorized so you can come whenever you want and stay as long as you like, right? If you keep ignoring the signs and someone finds out, you might not get authorized."

"But going in the *opposite* direction is just plain silly!" Dylan replied shortly, and continued down the path. Clare did not argue and walked with him in silence.

Soon, however, their path stopped in front of a high wall with a gate. Dylan tried the gate. It would not open, but a small screen in the wall lit up. Words came onto the screen with these directions: "To open the gate, give proof of LIFE and insert your visitor's pass into the slot."

"What's that supposed to mean?" Dylan asked. "What does it want to do, take my pulse?" He found the slot and thrust his pass inside.

After a few seconds, the pass came back out. The screen lit up with these words: "Rejected. First-time visitor. Proof of LIFE required."

"Look how LIFE is in all capitals," Clare pointed out. "Maybe LIFE is a place that other path leads to. Maybe once we get there, we get some kind of stamp on our pass or something."

This made some sense to Dylan, but before he could answer, Clare pointed at the screen. "Look," she said, "it's saying something else."

Dylan looked. The letters had changed and now the screen read: "Warning. Attempts to ignore posted signs may result in permanent loss of visitor's passes."

Dylan gave up. "All right. I guess there's no other choice. We're going to have to waste who-knows-how-much of our four days going in the *opposite* direction from where we can see we ought to go." He cast one last, longing look at the city with its rich jewel colors and turned his back on it. Together, the cousins began to retrace their steps. Before long, Dylan and Clare were back where they had started, at the first sign pointing the way for first-time visitors.

They passed the sign and followed the road through the woods, then across a grassy meadow, and up a little hill. From the top of this hill, Dylan and Clare could see another hill across from them. Nestled between the two hills lay what appeared to be a garden park. In the park, a footpath wound through tall, stately cypress trees. Stone statues and small markers dotted the park's open spaces. Twisting up and over many of the statues, ropes of ivy grew wild and untended. Near many of the markers, golden flowers added flecks of color. A black wrought iron fence enclosed the whole park, its gate standing open. Dylan and Clare's path led through this gate. Pointing in, one more sign read, "FIRST-TIME VISITORS. THIS WAY."

The cousins descended the hill and passed through the gate. "This is all very pretty," Dylan muttered, "but I really didn't want to visit a garden. I wanted to get to Holiday."

"It is pretty," Clare agreed, "and peaceful. Almost too peaceful. It feels very serious, like a place for having some kind of ceremonies." She and Dylan were walking on the footpath now, as it wound in and out among the trees. The only path to be seen, it led the two deeper and deeper into the garden, toward the base of the second hill, where it appeared to dead end. Once they reached the base of that hill, though, Dylan and Clare found that the path continued, leading into a rounded opening that had been cut in the rock.

Dylan and Clare peered into this entrance. The path seemed to go straight back, through a long hallway or tunnel, into the hill itself. Clare looked at Dylan. "So what do we do now?" she asked.

"I guess we go in," he answered. "The sign at the gate said, 'First-time visitors, this way.' There's no other path. This must be where we go."

"Are you sure that's wise?" a man's voice asked.

Dylan jumped. He turned to see where the voice had come from. Off to the side, on a bench half hidden by a bush, Mr. Smith sat watching Dylan and Clare.

"I didn't see you there," Dylan said, once he got over his surprise. He held up his green visitor's pass. "Are you using one of these too?"

Mr. Smith stood up and came over to Dylan and Clare. He flashed his usual pleasant smile. "Oh," he said, "are we talking about going to the *real* Holiday again?" He looked around. "Are we there now? Is this it?" And he smiled again.

"No, this isn't it," Dylan said, "but all the signs point this way. They say first-time visitors need to come this way first. You must have seen the city when you came down the path."

"So you *haven't* been to the real Holiday?" the man asked.

Dylan and Clare shook their heads. "Not yet," Clare said.

Mr. Smith nodded. "Of course not," he said. Another pleasant smile. Then he said, as if to himself, "Children always want a bigger and better Holiday." He shook his head. Then he put his hand on Dylan's shoulder and gazed into his eyes. "There's only one way to have a bigger and better Holiday," he said earnestly, "and that is by hanging on to the good feelings and the brotherly spirit you have while you're in the Holiday we visit on vacation. Some day, when you're older,

you'll understand that." He let go of Dylan's shoulder and gave it a little pat.

"But for now," Mr. Smith said, "I heard you say you were going to go through that doorway. It's okay to be childish sometimes—it's charming, really—but even children should understand about safety."

Dylan peered through the doorway again. "What's unsafe about it?" he asked. "It's a good, wide path; it's even paved. It just goes straight; you couldn't get lost. And there's plenty of light."

The little man, usually so good-natured, had become quite serious. "I don't like to scare you," he said gently, "but you really mustn't go in there. Many people have, but far fewer have come out." And he shook his head sadly.

"Why?" Dylan asked. "*Why* don't they come out?"

"They get in there and they get stuck," Mr. Smith replied. "They're not able to get back out again."

"If it's that dangerous, why do all the signs point in and say that's the way to go?" Dylan asked. "There aren't any warning signs."

The man looked into Dylan's face and muttered, "Poor, innocent child." Then, to Dylan, "It's never occurred to you that someone might be playing a trick on you?"

"That would be a pretty nasty trick!" Clare protested. "Deliberately trying to get someone to do something dangerous!"

Mr. Smith turned and looked her full in the face. He nodded. "Exactly my point," he said. Then he added, "I have to go now. But please, take my advice. Don't go in there." He raised his hand briefly, in a sad gesture of farewell, as if afraid he might not see them again. Then he turned and walked back along the path leading out of the park.

Dylan watched him go, then said to Clare, "You're right. That man *is* strange."

"More than just strange," Clare said, with a shiver. "He gives me the creeps."

"Oh, I don't think he means any harm," Dylan said. "He's just odd."

"What was all that scary stuff about going through the door?" Clare insisted.

"Maybe he really believes all that," Dylan answered. He peered through the doorway once more. "It's true that you can't see how far it goes."

"Maybe we *shouldn't* go in," Clare said.

"It must be okay," Dylan assured her. "These are official signs, and they point this way. Plus look at how well they maintain the path. Come on; we'll be fine. If we don't like it, we can always turn around and come back out."

Together, the cousins stepped over the threshold and through the door in the rock. Dylan expected the dampness and the mustiness. What took him by surprise was the immediate sense of having entered some place foreign. The familiar world of sunshine, trees, and singing birds was only one step behind him—he even glanced over his shoulder to make sure that was still the case—yet it seemed ages since he had been out there. Still, there at their feet, the broad, well-maintained path led on. Dylan began to walk, and Clare followed.

"I wonder how many visitors actually make it to Holiday if this is how they have to get there!" Clare's cheerful words sounded out-of-place in the silence.

Dylan knew she was trying to keep up her courage, and answered her in the same light tone. "I don't think our friend Strange Man will try it," he said. But his comment, too, seemed inappropriate, as if someone had made a joke, right out loud, in the middle of a funeral. Both children fell silent and made no further attempt at conversation. On they walked until the doorway was just a small glimmer of light behind them. The pathway actually grew broader the farther they walked. It appeared very well traveled. Eventually, smaller trails began to branch off, but since they were small and unpaved, it was impossible to mistake them for the main road.

The first moan Dylan heard came so softly that, once it died away, he convinced himself that he had never heard it. The next moan was also quiet, so quiet that he thought Clare had just sighed. The third moan, though still quiet, was definitely a moan, and it caused Dylan to say, "Clare? What's wrong?"

"Me?" Clare whispered back. "I thought you were making that noise."

Then it came again, a long, drawn-out shuddering groan. Now that it was louder, Dylan could tell that it came from off to the right somewhere. It must be far away, he thought, and he found that comforting.

"It's not an animal, is it?" Clare whispered.

"I'm sure it's a person," Dylan answered.

"I think I'd feel better if it were an animal," Clare said. The noise came again, still louder, sounding like a wolf's howl in the dead of night, yet decidedly human. Then another wail came and another, each fuller of grief and despair than the last. Whatever was making that noise had experienced something sadder than the saddest story Dylan had ever heard. The deathly stillness after each wail only made the next one more terrible.

"Listen!" Clare whispered sharply. "There's a new one." Dylan listened. Sure enough, a new voice had begun to moan off in the distance on the other side. As if in answer, more cries, and then more, started up until mournful wailing surrounded them. "This is very creepy!" Clare muttered.

"But all that noise is far away," Dylan replied, trying to calm his own nerves along with hers. "And look, you can still see the doorway back there. And the path is still well kept along here, so people must go this way. Plus look how light it still is." Dylan had been struck by this before. There was still light. It was not a natural light, like sunlight, and it was not very bright, but it was adequate to see by. Dylan could see no source for the light, but there it was and it was a tremendous help.

The cousins walked on, neither of them wanting to make it worse by saying so, but both of them hoping they had not much farther to go. Dylan had been so distracted by the dreadful noises that he had failed to notice the odor that had been steadily growing as they progressed deeper in under the rock. Now this odor had become so strong that it finally forced him to notice. Just as he did, Clare whispered loudly, "Ugh! What is that awful smell?" A memory flashed into Dylan's mind, the memory of coming upon a dead rabbit in the field near his house. The rabbit had evidently died several days earlier and it had smelled terrible, with an odor very similar to what was all around them now.

"I can't take much more of this," Clare said, out loud, but quietly. Dylan heard a tremor in her voice. For a brief moment, he felt a surge of revulsion for this evil-sounding, evil-smelling place. He had to resist the impulse to turn and run back the way he had come. Unexpectedly, a different memory arose from who-knows-where, replacing the memory of the dead rabbit and offering a stark contrast to the current surroundings.

"Clare, Holiday is just as wonderful as this is awful—more wonderful," Dylan said urgently. He spoke quietly, but he no longer whispered. Clare would not have been able to hear a whisper over the distant moans that were coming in constant, loud waves. "It smells awful in here, but I remember the smells from Holiday. I've never smelled anything like them—not just smells, the *feeling*. And this moaning is horrible, but I remember the music I heard from Holiday. It wasn't just music—it was like people I wanted to be with forever calling me to come join them. I'm sure it's worth all this to get there. Once we're there, we'll forget about all this. I know we will."

Just then, all the moaning and all the wailing stopped. A dead silence that could almost be felt filled the tunnel. And then one long, piercing, terrified shriek rang out. Was the screamer a male or a female? Was it a child or an adult? Dylan could only have said that, again, it was a human. Surely, it was a human who had come face-to-face with the greatest of all horrors.

"That's it!" Clare whispered fiercely. "I don't think I can take this."

And before Dylan could reply, Clare turned on her heel, and took two quick steps back the way they had come. Dylan saw her hesitate, then step to the right, then to the left. She seemed to be looking for something she could not see. Then Clare stopped altogether and came slowly back to where Dylan stood. She was crying.

"What is it?" Dylan asked.

"The opening is gone," Clare replied in a lifeless monotone of despair.

"No, it's not. I can see it back there," Dylan answered, and he turned to face the entrance into the tunnel, way back in the distance. As he turned to face it, though, the entrance disappeared. In its place was an unbroken rock wall. Not only that, but the path they had taken disappeared as well. Since the way had become so wide, Dylan could not even tell where in the distant wall the opening had been. "How can that be?" Dylan said to himself. He turned back around, facing away from where the opening had been, and looked over his shoulder. When he looked over his shoulder like this, the hole in the rock was there, leading out into daylight. Dylan quickly turned to face the opening and, just as quickly, it disappeared once more.

"That must be what the man meant," Clare said in a shaky whisper. "We're not going to be able to get out."

The wailing recommenced. It began quietly, but quickly grew to full strength once more. It sounded even more desolate than before.

Dylan tried to resist the rising tide of panic he felt inside. "Well, maybe we can't get out that way, but we're not supposed to go that way," he said, sounding much more certain than he felt. "Look up here." He pointed ahead. "See how the path goes down into that—chamber, or whatever you call it. I'll bet that's the way out."

Clare had grabbed Dylan's hand. "I don't like it," she said. "We can't see where it goes. And look how narrow it is. We'd have to go one at a time. I don't want to go without you."

"Look, Clare," Dylan said, "you can stand right here by where it starts to go down, and I'll go first. I'll see what's there and come back and tell you."

"I don't want to wait here by myself," Clare insisted. "And what if whoever screamed is down there?"

Dylan did not want to think about that. "I'll only go down a few steps," Dylan promised. "Then I'll come right back. It will just take a minute."

Clare, frightened as she was, could still see that there was no other choice. Reluctantly, she let go of Dylan's hand, and he started down. The path quickly turned into something more like a series of uneven steps. The descent was not difficult, but it wound slightly, something like a spiral staircase. After twelve steps, Dylan still could not see what lay around the next corner or how far down the steps led. He did not want to turn back without knowing more, but, aware of Clare waiting, frightened, above him, he turned back to tell her it looked easy and she should come right behind him.

The problem was that, when he turned around, the twelve steps he had already descended were nowhere to be seen.

Dylan felt that he'd been tricked. "Why didn't I think of that?" he thought to himself. Just as the doorway into the tunnel had disappeared when they had turned back toward it, so the stairs had now disappeared for Dylan. When he tried to go back up them, they were gone. He found himself standing at the top of a series of steps (instead of at the twelfth one down), a solid wall behind him and a low ceiling above. There was no way back to Clare.

Dylan felt more alone than he had ever felt in his life. "Clare!" he called as loudly as he could. "Clare! Can you hear me?" The stone absorbed his voice so that even to him it sounded muffled and faint. He heard no answer from Clare. As he listened, he realized that he no longer heard any moans or wails either. He stood surrounded by silence as deep as that of the tomb. And it was growing dark on the steps.

Dylan did not know what else to do, except to keep moving down. So down he went. Perhaps this really was the way out. If he could get out the other end of the tunnel, surely he could find a way to go back in from the front and find Clare. Or perhaps, when he did not come back up, Clare would come down looking for him. Maybe she was following him right now and he just could not see her. Hoping so, Dylan went on down the steps. Down, down, down he went. Twice, Dylan turned around to see if the steps he had just come down were still there. They were not.

At last, Dylan reached the bottom. All the way down, there had been light on the steps so Dylan could see to walk. But as he stepped on to the stone floor at the bottom of the steps, the light went out completely. Darkness swallowed everything. Dylan reached immediately behind him, to touch the last steps he had just descended. As he had feared, he could feel no steps, only a solid rock wall. He put his arms in front of him and took a few cautious steps—only a few, because he came to another solid rock wall. Dylan felt along the wall to the right. It went a few feet, then turned, and Dylan felt more rock. It took Dylan only a few seconds to fully understand his situation. He was deep under the ground, in a pitch-dark chamber of rock just big enough to lie down in, completely cut off from everyone and everything. There was no way out.

4

The Forest of Life

*H*orror—the stark realization that the unimaginable has happened to *you*. Despair—the dark, black certainty that there is no room for hope.

Horror and despair—Dylan knew nothing else. These two things were his whole world. *How long had he been here?* he wondered dully. Forever, it seemed. His parents, the vacations in Holiday, Clare, whom he had last seen in the half-lit cave—those were all things from a past so far distant that it must have been someone else's life and not Dylan's. His own existence had become very simple. It held room for nothing but terror and despair.

At first, Dylan had tried to keep hope alive. His parents knew he had headed for Holiday, and they would come looking for him. They would see all the signs that pointed the way for first-time visitors, and they would know which way he had gone. But then

Dylan remembered all the wails and moans he and Clare had heard. Those were surely the voices of people like him, lost in this black tomb, who had never been found. Dylan began to imagine his parents coming after him, wanting him back. He imagined them taking the same deceptive path he had followed. He saw them, too, being led down to their own little dark chamber, only to find, as he had, that the path led *in*, but no path led out.

Another wave of despair tugged at Dylan's mind and sucked him under. Nothing could be done. He was helpless to escape his prison. Nor could anyone else rescue him or even locate him. Dylan peered again into the darkness, but of course, he still could not see. (It was no consolation at all that there was nothing to be seen.) He strained to hear anything in the stillness—he would even have been glad to hear the hideous moans again—but he could hear only a deathly silence. And that humming.

Humming? Dylan lifted his head to hear better. Yes, from somewhere, a faint hum penetrated his prison walls. How long had there been humming? He was certain that it had not just begun, that it had been going on for a while, but he distinctly remembered a time when he had not been able to hear it. He could hear it now, however, and whatever it was, he welcomed it. The sound delighted Dylan, because it meant there was at least one other thing in his world besides horror and despair.

Where had Dylan heard a sound like this before? Maybe it was like the sound of the surf at the beach, only softer. No, not quite that—it was the sound of wind in the forest. That was it! The hum sounded like a breeze in the top of pine trees, except for this: every now and then, in the hum, Dylan thought he heard a word. Dylan kept listening—after all, he had nothing else to do—and the longer he listened, the more certain he grew that the humming contained words. At first, the only words he could pick out were plant kinds of words, like "forest," "ivy," "wither," "tree," "grow," and "evergreen." As he continued to listen, though, he began to hear other kinds of words as well—"die" and "winter," "life" and "everlasting."

Dylan felt he could listen, content, to the humming forever. The relief at knowing something else *was*, even it if was outside his prison's walls, was that great. Then came the voice. Dylan did not recognize it as belonging to anyone he knew. Yet, though he had never heard it before, it seemed somehow familiar. If Dylan had tried to describe it, he would have said the voice was *huge*, the biggest voice he'd ever heard. Indeed, the voice filled Dylan's little black chamber, leaving no space for anything else. The voice called Dylan's name, once, then fell silent.

Dylan jumped to his feet, heart pounding. Someone knew he was here after all. Someone had come to get him out. "I'm here! I'm in here!" Dylan called. The darkness and the stone dwarfed his own voice and swallowed it. He tried again, louder. "I'm here! I'm in here! It's me! Dylan!" No answer. "It's me, Dylan," he called again, "the one you're looking for!" He paused and listened. He heard only the humming with its occasional words—no voice, no approaching footsteps. He yelled and yelled without a response, then, finally, his despair deeper than ever, Dylan sank back down onto the floor, his back against the cave wall.

"Dylan!" came the huge voice again, and, again, Dylan jumped to his feet. He could not help it. It simply was not possible to remain sitting in the presence of that voice. "Come this way," the voice commanded, then fell silent. From those few simple words, Dylan understood two things. He knew he must obey that voice. Nothing less than his complete and precise obedience would do. And he knew he must meet the one who had spoken.

Almost immediately, Dylan heard another little voice, from inside his own head. Dylan knew he had heard this voice before, although it was not until later that he realized where. "Come where?" this voice said quietly, but indignantly. "There's nothing here but four solid stone walls. You can't 'come' anywhere!" From experience, Dylan knew that this second voice told the truth, but it did not matter to him. He had to obey the huge voice, whether he could or not. He had no choice. He walked forward, feeling for the wall that he knew was right in front of his face—but it was not there. He took another step, then another, still feeling for a wall, but he never found one. He walked on in the direction from which the voice had called, the hum growing louder with each step he took. He had not walked very far at all when he saw bright daylight pouring in at an opening just ahead. He headed for that opening—the hum had become quite loud now—and stepped at last through a hole in the stone just his size and out into a forest clearing.

Nothing in Dylan's life had ever smelled as wonderful as the fragrance of these pines. Nothing had ever felt so delicious as the warm breeze playing with the grass in the clearing. Nor had anything ever appeared so alive as this great, green, growing forest. For a moment, Dylan did nothing but soak up the richness of ordinary, everyday life. Then, suddenly, he realized how badly his legs were shaking, and he sank down onto the forest floor.

Reminded by his shaky legs of the danger he had just escaped, Dylan looked around for the possessor of the voice that had called his name and led him out. He saw no one. And as for the humming, he was sure that it was not just the wind in the trees he had been hearing, because the occasional words had become even more distinct. Who had called him and what was making the humming song? And most importantly—Dylan went cold all over as the thought came to him—where was Clare?

To Dylan's credit, as soon as he remembered Clare, he jumped to his feet and headed back toward the hideous darkness he had just left. A voice something between a squeak and a loud whisper stopped him in his tracks. "Where you goin'?" the voice asked. "You can't go back in, you know. And why would you want to anyway? People never want to go back in once they're out."

Dylan turned around. He could see no one. There were only the trees surrounding the small clearing in front of the cave's opening. "Who are you? Where are you?" Dylan called loudly.

For a moment, a squeaky, breathy laugh was the only response. It reminded Dylan of the times when he and Clare would begin giggling at the dinner table, when they were younger, and find themselves unable to stop. Waiting for the laughter to subside gave Dylan time to look for its source. It really seemed to be coming from a small fir tree on the edge of the clearing, a tree not much taller than Dylan. No breeze of any kind blew any of the other trees at the moment, but this one little tree shook and rustled, *Just like a tree might do if it were laughing*, Dylan thought to himself.

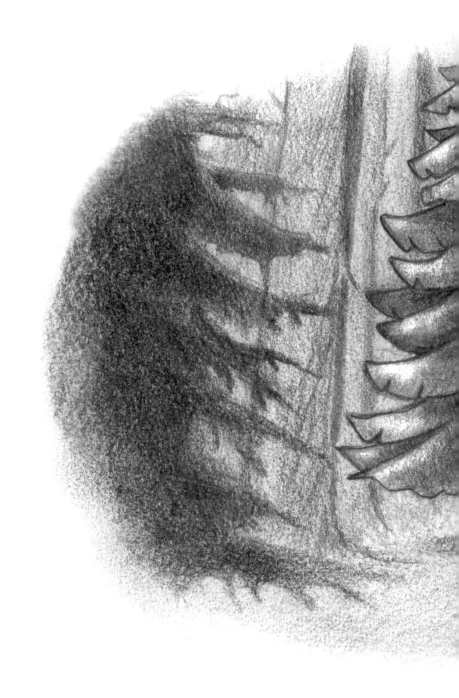

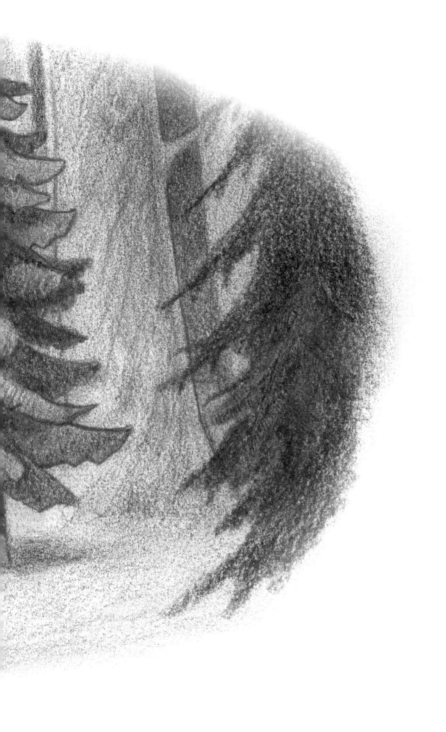

At last the tree (for by now Dylan felt sure that this was, indeed, who laughed) gave a long shudder and sighed. "Whew! Sorry," it said, with the voice of someone who has finally pulled himself together enough to speak. "I didn't mean to laugh at you. It was just so funny to see you yelling when I'm right in front of you."

Dylan's anxiety for Clare made him a bit sharp. "You can't blame me for not expecting a *tree* to be the one talking."

Completely serious now, the tree replied, "Really? Don't they talk where you come from?"

"Of course not," Dylan almost snapped, then, thoughtfully, "at least, *I've* never heard one."

"Aha!" the tree crowed. "That's not at all the same thing, is it? Is it that the trees don't talk? Or is it that you don't hear?"

A thought occurred to Dylan. "Then, *was* the song I heard coming from the trees?" Before the tree could reply, though, Dylan shook his head. "You know, I really don't care right now," he said. "My cousin's back in there, lost, and I need to go find her."

"Dad!" called the talking tree, and from behind it came another voice, larger, deeper, husky.

"*You* can't find her," this deeper voice said. "And if you could, you couldn't get her out through *your* exit. She has to come out her own exit."

"Her own exit?" Dylan looked, puzzled, at the tall fir tree who was speaking. It stood just behind and to the left of the younger, giggly tree. "How many exits to that cave are there?"

"Oh, there are as many exits as there are people who come out," the tree replied. "Everyone has his or her own exit; there are no two alike. But every exit leads out into this forest, so you're sure to meet up with her again. In fact, someone's coming now. Down in my roots, I can feel footsteps coming this way."

Dylan waited, holding his breath. Soon, he could hear the footsteps the tree felt and, an instant later, he saw the person making them. "Clare!" he called, and ran to her. Dylan and Clare were not the kind of cousins that embraced every time they saw each other, but they hugged one another tightly now. Dylan thought he heard the young tree whisper, "I wish I could do that with *my* branches."

"Have you been out of the cave long?" Dylan asked his cousin.

Clare nodded. "For a while. Oh, Dylan, I am *so* glad to see you! I was afraid you'd never come out. How did you get out?" she asked. Something must have been in her eye, because she had to rub at it for a moment.

Dylan told Clare about the steps that had led him deep into the dark hole and had then disappeared, preventing him from going back up again. He told her how hopeless and how helpless he had felt, sitting alone in his little space of darkness. He told how, first, he had heard the humming, and then a voice that had called him. "It was the strangest thing," he tried to explain. "When that voice called, 'Come,' I had to do it, even though I knew I couldn't. And as soon as I began moving toward it, there was nothing stopping me at all. I went just a little ways and then here I was, in this for-est. Hey! Do you realize these trees can talk? At least some of them can."

Clare laughed. "Yes, I've been talking with trees, too," she said.

"Not to sound mushy," Dylan said, "but it sure is good to hear you laugh! I didn't know how I was going to find you in there. In fact, the tree here told me I wouldn't be able to. He said you'd have your own exit and you wouldn't be able to use mine. How did *you* get out?"

"Well, I heard the humming too," Clare said, "only it wasn't coming from outside anywhere; it was inside my own head. I noticed it just as soon as I couldn't see you anymore, so I was never really afraid. I just stood there waiting—remember, it wasn't as dark where I was—and I listened to the humming so I wouldn't feel scared. And you know what I realized about the humming? I've been hearing it all my life, at least as far back as I can remember. I remember Mom and Dad humming it to me, when I was tiny. It's one of the earliest memories I have. Anyway, I listened to the humming and didn't worry. And I'm sure I heard the same voice you did, only for me, it wasn't a separate loud voice. It was just mixed in with the humming—like it was part of the humming, but separate too. Pretty soon, I realized from the humming that I was supposed to walk straight ahead and that would lead me out. I didn't want to go at first, because I was worried about you. But I felt really sure that I needed to go and that someone else would take care of you. There was nothing I could do for you. So I followed the path and came out into the forest."

Dylan turned to the trees who had spoken with him earlier. "What about all the other people in the cave?" he wanted to know. "We heard all kinds of horrible moaning and wailing—will they all find their own exits and get out too?"

"In the first place," the tree spoke patiently, as if explaining something to a little child, "no one *finds* his or her exit. People

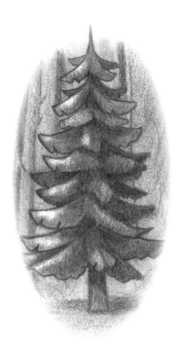

have to be *brought* to their exits. And then, no, not everyone will get out. Not everyone pays attention to the humming."

Dylan found this hard to believe. "Why not?" he asked.

A breeze—or something—rustled through the tall tree's upper branches, as though it had shrugged. "Some of the people in there don't believe the humming is real. Other people don't even notice it. Who knows what all the reasons are, but one thing's certain—though many people go in, far fewer come out."

Dylan turned to Clare. "That's just what that man said—you know, the one who keeps trying to talk us out of seeing the real Holiday, Mr. Smith." Dylan's eyes widened as he realized something. "Clare!" he said. "It was *his* voice. When the big voice called me to come out, there was something in my head telling me I couldn't, that there was no way out. I didn't really pay much attention to it, because I was so focused on the big voice. *But it was that man's voice* that was telling me it was impossible. It was inside my own head, but I know it was his voice!"

Dylan turned back to the trees. "Who called me to come out of the cave?" he asked. "Was it a tree?"

The younger tree exploded in a burst of laughter. It shook all over as if at the mercy of a violent storm. The laughter continued for a full minute. The little tree's father made several embarrassed attempts at stopping it, saying things like, "All right, that's enough," and "Come on, now, calm down."

The laughter subsided at last with a final, "Oh my." Then the little tree said quietly, as though to himself, "What does he think we are—*magic* trees?" and he giggled again.

"The Founder called you," the older tree responded in a glad and grave voice.

The horror of the cave, the terror of thinking he would never leave it, the relief at finding himself outside, and the joy of reunion with Clare—all these had driven thoughts of Holiday clear out of Dylan's mind. Now, with the mention of the Founder, desire for the real Holiday flooded over him again, with even greater intensity. His experiences in the cave, rather than discouraging him in his quest for the real Holiday, made him that much more certain that it must be well worth the price.

"The Founder," Dylan repeated softly. If he was the owner of the big voice, Dylan wanted to find him more than ever. "Does the Founder live here in this forest?"

That set the little tree off again. "You must think this is a pretty big forest, if you think that it could hold the Founder!" it managed to gasp, in between outbursts.

Dylan had begun to feel somewhat annoyed with the little tree's giggling fits. Its father felt the same way, apparently, for it now said, sternly, "That's enough. This is really not the time to be silly."

"I can't help it," the tree protested, "he has such funny ideas."

"You will help it," the father tree replied, "or I won't let the squirrels play in your branches when they come later today."

That produced an instant effect. The little tree made a noise as though it were choking on something—*another burst of laughter*, Dylan thought—then grew silent. A slight tremble in its branches gave the only evidence of how great an effort this cost the little tree.

The older tree turned its attention back to Dylan. "The Founder doesn't live here," he told him. "This is his forest, though. He's the one who planted it, right up against that cave. People who keep Holiday—and even many who don't—enjoy the trees of this forest."

Dylan and Clare turned to each other, their faces lit with the same idea that had just occurred to them both. "The trees on the way into Holiday," Clare said.

"The ones that seem to smell more pine-y and to look more beautiful than trees at home," Dylan added.

The little tree spoke up, its fits of silliness over for now. "They're from here," it said with pride. "Trees from the Forest of Life. All the trees in this forest are evergreens, and only evergreens. Pine trees, fir trees—trees that never lose their leaves and look dead. We're evergreen trees; we are *ever* green, alive all the time, even in the dead of winter. We're Forest of

Life trees, we are," and the little tree seemed to draw itself up to be an inch or two taller.

"Oh, then maybe this was where we were supposed to go," Dylan said. "We were trying to get to the city of Holiday—the real one, you know, not just the fake one that we always go to for vacations—and we got to a gate we couldn't open. There was a sign that said we needed Proof of LIFE—was it talking about this forest?"

The young tree emitted the tiniest trace of a giggle, but quickly got it under control. "This *is* where you're supposed to be and some little proof that you've been here is *exactly* what you need."

"What kind of proof?" Dylan asked, looking around him.

"Cut off a piece from one of my branches," the father tree suggested. "Don't worry—that's one way plants are better than people. Cut a piece off of you, and it's a real problem—cut a piece off of a plant and the plant just grows better. Here, look, this little bit of branch right here," and it waved a branch.

Dylan took out his penknife and did as the tree said, although he could not help feeling that there was something wrong with cutting a piece from a tree that could talk. The tree, however, did not seem to mind in the least. Dylan put the piece of branch in his backpack, and asked, "And where do we go from here? You already said no one goes back into that cave once they're out; how do we get back on our way to the real Holiday?"

"Go straight on through the Forest, and you'll find, when the trees begin to grow scarce, a little winding bit of a road that will lead right to that same gate that required proof of life. Once you're through that gate, you'll find yourself in a part of a town that you won't much like. It's not Holiday, that's for sure, but another little town just on the outskirts. Stay alert and watch out, because it's not a safe place."

"Is that the only way to get there?" Clare asked.

"It is for first-time visitors," the tree answered. "Your goal is a pretty little park in that part of town. If you keep following the widest path, you can't miss it. It's a very pretty park, and perfectly safe, despite its surroundings. You can spend the night there quite comfortably."

"Will the Founder be there?" Dylan asked. "Because that's what I really want—to find the Founder so I can be authorized to get into Holiday whenever I like. And," he added, "to thank him for getting me out of the cave."

The little tree corrected him. "You don't find the Founder; he finds you. He's not just the Founder; he's the Finder too." The tree giggled, just a little. "That rhymed."

"I know," Dylan said. "I've heard it before."

"But remember," the father tree said, ignoring all the interruptions, "you must have a visitor's pass or you can't get into the park. And if you don't get in the park, you might as well turn around and go back home."

"Not a problem. We have visitor's passes," Dylan said, holding his up.

"No, but you have to have one when you get to the park," the little tree said.

The big tree leaned over so that it was touching the smaller tree. "Don't worry about it," it said. "They'll have what they need when they get there."

"Well, thank you," Dylan said, starting off.

"Yes, you've been tremendously helpful," said Clare.

"And thanks for the piece of branch," Dylan added, but he couldn't be heard. The little tree could contain itself no longer and was laughing hysterically once more. "Did you hear what she said?" it was gasping. "We've been tremendously helpful. Get it? *Tree*-mendously!" And it roared with laughter.

5

Places of Evil

hose trees give a whole new meaning to the words, 'living plants,'" Dylan said, as he and Clare walked on through the forest.

"And the whole forest is like that," Clare replied. "It's like when you're in the woods right after it rains and you see big drops hanging on the ends of everything, just waiting to fall. This forest is like that, only instead of drops of water ready to fall, it's dripping with—well, with 'alive-ness,' if you know what I mean."

The cousins walked for a moment in silence, then Clare said, "In fact, I'll be sorry when we're out of this forest. The next place doesn't sound nearly so nice."

"True," Dylan agreed, "but I'm sure it's okay or the trees wouldn't have sent us that way. Hey, look, isn't that the gate up there?"

And sure enough, Dylan and Clare were coming out of the forest and were back at the gate that had refused them entrance earlier. This time, when Dylan inserted his pass and the gate asked for "Proof of LIFE," he waved the pine branch near the screen. The gate clicked and swung open. The children stepped through.

Immediately inside the gate stood a bench next to a bright green stand with a box at the top. Large letters on the box's lid said, "TAKE ONE." Dylan opened the box and took one of the papers that were inside.

"Maybe it's more directions about where to go," Clare said.

"Not exactly," said Dylan, reading the paper and seating himself on the bench. Clare sat too, and Dylan began to read out loud. "It says 'Holiday' at the top," he began, "then it says:

AUTHORIZED PERSONNEL WILL:

- look out for the interests of others, not just for their own personal interests;
- pay back good for evil;
- do, speak, and think only what is kind;
- keep tempers, emotions, and mouths under control at all times;
- demonstrate forgiveness to the same person up to 490 times;
- show all due respect to the Founder of Holiday;
- rejoice in the very fullest way possible.

Dylan sat for a moment, grunted, "Hm," then got up to return the flyer to the box.

"Don't you think we should hang on to it?" Clare suggested.

"I guess so," Dylan answered, folding the paper and putting it in his shirt pocket. Then he began to walk on down the path.

Just as the tree had said, now that Dylan and Clare were inside the gate, they found themselves in the narrow streets and dirty sidewalks of a not-so-nice part of what seemed a not-so-nice town. Concrete covered almost everything, resulting in a dull gray sameness wherever one looked. Passers-by had scrawled their names and other words in large, painted letters on the dirty buildings. In spite of the occasional trash barrel, wrappers, bottles, and cups littered the ground.

"The tree was certainly right about one thing," Dylan said. "I *don't* like this part of town. But following the widest path is easy enough, and hopefully that park's not too far off."

"But let's hurry," said Clare. "The sun will be going down soon. I really don't want to get caught here in the dark."

The two quickened their steps. Some of the people on the sidewalks also walked with quick steps. These people seemed preoccupied with business of their own and paid little attention to anyone else. For the most part, they walked alone. Occasionally, two of them hurried along together, but without speaking to each other. A man in a business suit almost collided with Dylan, but Dylan jumped aside. "No, tomorrow's not good enough!" the man growled into a cell phone that he held in one hand. His other hand, curled into a fist, struck the air angrily. "It's today or you can just forget it!" The man went on his way. He did not seem to have even noticed Dylan.

Some people wandered about in small groups, apparently with no destination, or stood slouching in the road. They laughed and made inaudible comments to one another while staring boldly at strangers passing by. These people seemed to feel a need for excitement, and Clare felt their need would only be met by doing some kind of mischief. From behind her, Clare heard a crash and the tinkling of broken glass. She jumped and turned around. Dylan did too. Two boys ran, laughing, from a storefront window with a hole in it. An old man in an apron was coming out of the door of the store, shaking his fist. "You punks!" he called. "You'll laugh in the back of a police car!" No sooner had the old man said this than a police car tore around the corner and squealed to a halt in front of the boys, blocking their path. Two uniformed men jumped from the car, seized the startled boys by the arms, clubbed them over the head with sticks several times, then forced them into the car. The car drove away.

"What was that?" Dylan asked.

"I don't know who to feel sorry for," Clare said, "the old man or the boys! Aren't policemen supposed to read people their rights, or something?"

"Maybe those rules don't apply here," Dylan suggested. "Let's keep moving. I'm with you that the sooner we're out of here, the better."

Dylan and Clare went on. At one point, their path led them right between two of the groups of slouching loafers. The two groups stood on opposite sidewalks. They eyed one another across the street and smiled mocking, dangerous smiles. Dylan and Clare hurried past, not wanting to be there when the storm that seemed to be brewing in these loiterers should break.

Still following the widest path, the cousins turned a corner. The scenery changed abruptly. "This is better," said Clare, relieved. This street led past green well-kept lawns where large houses flaunted impressive doors and large, imposing windows.

Fences, some wrought iron, some made of stone, others wooden, enclosed every house. Each fence had at least one sign reading, "PRIVATE PROPERTY. KEEP OUT." Some fences also had signs reading, "KEEP OFF THE GRASS" or "NO TRESPASSING. VIOLATORS WILL BE PROSECUTED."

"Or maybe it's not so much better," Clare added. "Something's wrong with this neighborhood."

"It's loud, for one thing," Dylan said. "You'd expect a neighborhood that looks like this one to be quiet and peaceful."

"Well, it certainly isn't!" said Clare. And it certainly wasn't. From some houses, televisions and stereos blared at highest volume. From many houses, angry voices could be heard. From one open window, Dylan and Clare heard the raised voices of a man and woman.

"Who asked you anyway?" the man's voice roared. "I didn't marry you so you could boss me around."

"Yeah?" shrilled back a woman's voice. "What did you marry me for, then? Because for the life of me, I can't imagine what *I* was thinking when I married *you*!" At that, a curse word rang out, along with the sound of something being smashed. The children hurried on down the sidewalk.

"Look out!" Dylan cried in a sharp tone.

Clare jumped back so that the flashy sports car just missed her. Its driver was backing at top speed out of his driveway, which crossed the sidewalk. His eye caught Clare and, instead of stopping to apologize, as the children expected, the driver leaned from the window of his car and yelled, "Watch where you're goin'!"

"One thing I think we can say for sure," Dylan said. "These people are certainly not part of Holiday's authorized personnel! Remember that list of requirements?" And he pulled it from his pocket and read, "'Do, speak, and think only what is kind; keep tempers, emotions, and mouths under control at all times.' Wherever this is, it must not be part of Holiday."

The sidewalk led past a park, where two groups of boys with bats were choosing teams. Dylan heard a clear voice snap, "I don't want *him* on my team; he can't even hit the ball!" Dylan whipped his head around to see the speaker because something sounded so familiar. Of course, Dylan did not recognize the boy who had spoken, but when he looked at him, the boy looked back at Dylan and held his gaze for a moment. Suddenly, Dylan realized what it was that he had heard before. It was not the speaker's voice; it was what he had said. The last time Dylan had played baseball with his friends, he had said those exact same words about Sam Parker. Was that how *he* had sounded? But Sam had never hit a ball in his life; why did he always want to play with the guys when they got together for baseball?

The houses looked a little less expensive now, although they still had the fences and the "Keep Out" signs. Dylan and Clare came up to a red light and stopped to wait for the "Walk" signal. Across from them, an old man in a motorized wheelchair and a teenage boy walking toward Dylan and Clare waited to cross as well. The light turned green, and Dylan and Clare stepped into the crosswalk. On the other side, the elderly man started first in his wheelchair, forcing the teenager to walk behind him until they had passed Dylan and Clare. "Come on, old man, could you go any *slower*?" the teenager called out.

Dylan's first reaction was one of shock that someone would say such a thing to an elderly man. Then, with an even greater shock, Dylan recognized the teenager's words as the very words he himself had said, not even a week ago! Oh, he had only muttered them under his breath, and the old man in question had not heard them, but they had been the exact same words. "Come on, old man, could you go any *slower*?" Even though the old man had not heard Dylan at the time, his friend Danny, who was with him, had heard and had laughed—which was just what Dylan had hoped for. Then Dylan got his third shock. The old man was just at the point of passing Dylan and Clare, so Dylan could clearly see the spiteful grin that spread across his face at the teenager's words.

"I'll take all the time I want, kid, and I don't care who has to wait!" the old man said.

"Nice place," Clare muttered, but Dylan did not answer. He was too stunned by the way two strangers in a row had said the exact words he remembered saying himself. For one thing, the coincidence was just too weird; but for another thing, hearing these things said right out loud by other people made him see how nasty they really sounded. And then it happened again. They passed a church whose doors were open, with well-dressed people entering. A mom, a dad, and their son were coming from the parking lot, and the son was complaining, for all the world to hear. "Why do you always make me come?" he groused. "I hate coming! It's boring!" And once again, Dylan recognized himself. That was what he thought almost every Sunday.

The widest road, the one the tree had said to keep to, turned again, and Dylan and Clare were back in the part of town that was dirtier and run-down. Little groups of slouching people still loafed there, pointing at passersby and whispering. Shadows were growing long as the afternoon drew to a close. The cousins hurried.

When they first heard feet coming after them, they walked faster and tried to ignore them. The footsteps began to run, then, so they whirled around to see who followed. "Oh, it's just him," Clare said, as they both recognized the pleasant-faced man who had such an odd way of turning up wherever they went.

"It *is* you," Mr. Smith beamed. "I thought so, but it was hard to tell from the back. Bad part of town, this, isn't it?" he said, shaking his head. "Bet you're glad *you* don't live here and that *you're* not like these people." As always, the man's voice was friendly enough, but Dylan felt that the look Mr. Smith fixed on him was somehow accusing and mocking at the same time—as though he realized what shameful things Dylan kept hearing people say and realized, too, that Dylan had said or thought them all himself. Mr. Smith shook his head again. "This is what we get when we go looking for a real Holiday," he said. "There *is* no

such thing. The best we can do is just enjoy our vacations in Holiday once a year and hold on to the memories. What you see here is just what people are, everywhere, all the rest of the time."

"Oh, no!" Clare countered. "People in the real Holiday aren't like this—Dylan, show him your list," and Dylan reached, reluctant, for the flyer in his pocket.

The man waved his hand. "Oh, no, save yourself the trouble," he smiled. "I've seen the list—always kind, always keeping one's temper and mouth under control, thinking of other people, not just yourself—isn't that how it goes? Where are you possibly going to find people like that to live in such a place?" He winked at Dylan. "Do you think *you'll* get authorized?" He chuckled softly, then gave a friendly wave. "Maybe I'll see you again," and he went on ahead of Dylan and Clare.

"The nerve of that guy!" Clare said. "He was insulting you!" Dylan didn't answer. He was too unhappy. He had been thinking the very things Mr. Smith had implied—if, in order to be authorized for Holiday a person had to fit the requirements on the flyer in his pocket, it did not look like he, Dylan, would qualify. Would it be possible to convince the Founder—if he ever met him—that Dylan could see now how ugly some of his past actions and attitudes had been and that he was truly sorry? Would the Founder believe him if he promised he would never be like that again and would prove to be a credit to Holiday? Dylan hoped so with all his heart and moved on, Clare following, in the same direction the little man had gone.

Mr. Smith had moved quickly and was already far ahead, near one of the groups loitering on the sidewalk. He seemed to pause near the group; maybe he even spoke to its members. Then he turned a corner and disappeared from sight.

The group, comprising half a dozen boys near their own age, watched Dylan and Clare approach. The boys in the group said nothing, only smiled those little smiles that made Clare nervous. They had passed the group and Clare was slowly exhaling a sigh of relief when she heard Dylan cry, "Hey!" Turning to him, she saw that he held his hand to the back of his head, and a small dirt clod, exploded now into fragments, lay at his feet. Clare followed the direction of Dylan's eyes as he stared back at the group of boys, who laughed quietly together and watched him.

Before she could say anything to stop him, Dylan had called out, "Who threw that?"

One boy slouched forward. "Threw what?" he asked, holding out a dirt clod in one hand. "One of these? Oh. Guess it must have been me."

"Well, knock it off and leave me alone!" Dylan ordered. He paused, then turned to go on.

"Sure, I'll let you alone," the boy replied. "As soon I do this." Dylan and Clare heard the dirt clod whistle through the air, and Dylan felt as well as heard the thud when it hit his shoulder.

Every thing in Dylan's mind evaporated except rage. He turned back and charged the boy, grabbing him by the jacket and shoving him to the ground. The boy bounced back to his feet instantly. The other boys closed in around them in a circle, blocking Clare's vision so she could hardly see Dylan at all. In her anxiety for her cousin, Clare hopped back and forth from one foot to the other without noticing it. She looked up and could have cried for joy when she saw a police car coming around the corner. It pulled up with a squeal next to the boys, and a policeman jumped out, brandishing a stick. "All right, all right, break it up," he called out in a bored voice, hitting boys with his stick.

The boys scattered, trying to get out of reach of the flailing stick. One blow struck Dylan on the back and he cried out, "Ow," then said, "But, Officer, it wasn't my fault. They were throwing things at us."

"Yeah, yeah," the policeman said, already getting back in his car, "but you stopped to make something of it, right? You should just be glad I came along when I did; those guys would have had you for lunch," and he closed his car door and drove away.

"Come on, Dylan, hurry," Clare said, not wanting to be anywhere in sight when the gang of boys reconvened. Dylan saw the wisdom of this and hurried away with her, around the corner where the wide path led. Then Clare squealed with delight and relief. "Look, Dylan," she cried, "it's right there! The park the tree told us about!" Just ahead a small grassy park invited them to come in and stroll under its graceful trees and relax on its wrought iron benches. A tall white fence, also of wrought iron, encircled the park. The gate was closed. A banner hung on the fence, with the words, "First-time visitors enter here." In smaller letters were the words, "Visitor's pass required."

Dylan approached the gate, Clare right behind him. On the gate was another small screen, like the one they had encountered at the previous gate. Above this screen, a small sign read, "Absolutely no admittance without visitor's pass." On the screen itself, in letters glowing a bright green, Dylan saw the same list that he had in his shirt pocket.

Authorized Personnel will:

- look out for the interests of others, not just for their own personal interests;
- pay back good for evil;
- do, speak, and think only what is kind;
- keep tempers, emotions, and mouths under control at all times;
- demonstrate forgiveness to the same person up to 490 times;
- show all due respect to the Founder of Holiday;
- rejoice in the very fullest way possible.

The words under the screen read, "Type in your first and last names."

Dylan turned back to Clare. Without looking at her, he said, "I don't think they'll let me in. I don't meet those requirements."

"Well, try it and see," Clare urged.

Dylan typed in his name. The words on the screen changed to, "Welcome, Dylan. Insert your visitor's pass."

Dylan reached for the wallet in his back pocket, where he had placed his visitor's pass. His wallet was not there. He tried the other pocket. It was empty too. "My wallet's gone!" he said.

"Did you leave it in the forest?" Clare asked.

Dylan shook his head. "No, we used visitor's passes at the last gate, remember? I had it then, and I put it back in my pocket." Suddenly Dylan understood. "Those guys back there, with the dirt clods. They were just trying to distract me so they could get my wallet."

Clare remembered how the gang of boys had closed in a tight circle around Dylan before the policeman came. "That must be it," she said. "Did you have much money in there?"

Dylan shook his head. "But what about Holiday? I can't even get into the park without my visitor's pass. Look at yours. What does it say on it about what happens if you don't have one?"

Clare pulled out her visitor's pass and read, "Failure to present this pass when asked to do so will result in a costly fine, immediate expulsion from Holiday, and the forfeiture of all right to ever return." Dylan looked at her with a sickly expression. "Look at the screen," Clare said, pointing at it. "It's saying something else."

Dylan looked and read the words, "If you have no visitor's pass, press 'No.'"

Dylan pressed the No button. The screen changed again. Now it said, "Enormous fine due now." Those words, however, remained on the screen for only a few seconds. Then they gave way to these: "Paid in full. New pass issued." The machine began to click, and slowly a new pass slid out. Dylan took it and saw that it had his name on it. Although in every other way it was just the same as his old one, where the old one had said, "Visitor's Pass," this new one read, "Dylan's Pass."

Puzzled but elated, Dylan took the pass and inserted it into the proper slot. Clare began to do the same, but stopped, staring at the pass in her hand. "Dylan, look!" she gasped. Dylan looked at her pass and saw that it had changed. It no longer read "Visitor's Pass." Instead, he saw the bold letters of "Clare's Pass." Wondering, Clare inserted her pass. The gate swung open and the two entered the park.

6

Mistletoe and Nightmares

T he gate swung shut behind Dylan and Clare. They heard quiet clicking sounds as it locked automatically. They had no feelings of fear about being locked in, only a sense of safety in knowing that everyone else was locked out. "And none too soon, either," Clare said as the last ray of the sun set behind a building. "I wouldn't want to spend the night out there."

Dylan was distracted with the mystery of how he had entered. "But who paid my fine?" he asked. "And how did we get new passes?"

"Why, it was the Founder of course." The voice was quiet but crystal clear, and it sounded deeply soothing.

Dylan and Clare looked all around, but the park was small and it was easy to see that they were the only people there. "It must be one of the trees," Dylan

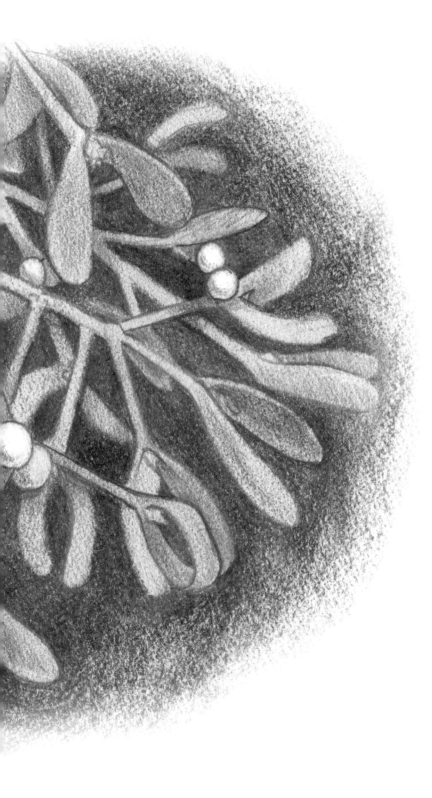

muttered under his breath to Clare. He began examining the closest one.

The voice laughed gently, a tinkling little laugh. "No, dear, not the tree," it said. "I'm growing *on* the tree."

The children looked and saw a mass of dark, leathery leaves hanging from one of the tree's branches, leaves that were clearly not the same as those of the tree itself. Dylan was thinking, *I've seen that kind of leaf before; where was it?* when Clare cried, "Mistletoe! You're a mistletoe plant!"

"That's right, dear," said the voice. "I'm Missy Mistletoe and I'm very pleased to meet you."

"I'm Clare," Clare said, "and this is my cousin, Dylan."

Having already had conversations with trees, the cousins did not waste much time in amazement that a mistletoe plant could speak. "Are you sure it was the Founder who paid my fine and got me the new pass?" Dylan asked.

"Of course it was," Missy answered so firmly that it was impossible not to believe her. "Who else is that generous and who else could possibly have paid such a huge fine?"

"Would it have been really big?" Dylan asked meekly.

"Oh my, yes, way out of your reach," Missy answered, "or anybody else's for that matter."

"So he wasn't mad that I lost my visitor's pass?" Dylan pressed.

"He very well might have been, but that wouldn't have stopped him," Missy said.

"I didn't *mean* to lose it," Dylan tried to explain.

Missy cut him short. "No one keeps his pass in that neighborhood. That's the main reason that the road goes through there."

"Clare didn't lose hers," Dylan protested.

"Clare's different," Missy answered. "She only had to come that way because she's traveling with you." Dylan started to ask why that would be so, but then it occurred to him that Clare's experience in the cave had been different from his as well, and he said nothing.

While Dylan puzzled over this, Clare had been thinking about something else. Now she said, "People decorate with mistletoe. They hang it in doorways and people kiss under it. Why is that?"

Missy gave her quiet tinkling laugh again. "It *is* a bit over-done sometimes, isn't it?" she said. "I'll have to tell you a bit of a story to answer that question. Why don't you have a seat on that bench?" The children sat and Missy began. "You know enough history to understand *why* Holiday exists, don't you?"

Dylan and Clare nodded. "A king got rid of the mean rulers it had, and the people who lived there turned the town into a kind of a monument to the king by making it as beautiful and happy a place as they could," Dylan said.

"Yes," said Missy. "But it was the townspeople's own fault that they needed to be liberated in the first place. The town had been ruled by a wise and generous Emperor, who lived in a faraway land and who supplied the town with everything it needed. The tyrants had come, pretending to have the best interests of the town at heart. They tricked the foolish citizens into rebelling against their rightful ruler, promising to take care of them and provide them with much better goods than the Emperor had ever given. When the good King came along, he showed the townspeople their mistake. They saw then that all the tyrants had given them was really bad for them. They realized they needed their Emperor. But the law was the law, and the law said that subjects who rebelled against the Emperor were cut off from him forever—unless they could pay a fine, a fine so huge there was no way in the world that the little town, devastated by years of oppression by bad rulers, could ever pay it. So the King, when he came, not only overthrew the tyrants and set the citizens free, he also paid the debt they owed the Emperor from his own purse."

"Was he that rich?" Dylan asked.

"Oh my, yes, you have no idea," Missy said.

"How much did he have to pay?" Dylan wanted to know.

"It cost him everything he had," Missy replied. "The Founder gave up everything to pay that debt. He became poorer than anyone else has ever been."

Baffled by such generosity, Dylan asked, "Why would he do that?"

"That's just how the Founder is," Missy said. "Why would he pay *your* fine?" Dylan had no answer for that, so Missy continued. "Long ago, in ancient times, when nations or towns who had been at war with each other patched up their quarrels and made peace, they often held the ceremony under a hanging piece of mistletoe. It was actually called the Plant of Peace. So people hang it everywhere in Holiday—downtown, in the Visitor's Center, in their homes. It reminds them that the citizens of the town have been reconciled to their Emperor. It's a tribute to the King who paid their debt and worked out the peace treaty." Then she added, "Of course, now *everyone* wants to kiss under the mistletoe."

Dylan agreed. "It actually gets a little sickening," he said.

Missy only laughed her little laugh again. Then she asked, "Are you hungry?" Dylan and Clare both suddenly realized that they were. "If you'll go to the back corner of the park, you'll find a box that has assorted cans and boxes of things that don't need to be cooked. Nothing fancy, but good healthy things that will keep you going. The Founder puts them there for people like you are who are passing through. You can save the food you brought in case you need it later. When you're finished eating, you'll find a stack of clean blankets in the same corner. The ground is soft here and the night is warm. A blanket under you and one on top and I think you'll be quite comfortable for the night."

Gratefully, Dylan and Clare made a simple but satisfying supper. They spread out the blankets and slipped off to sleep before they had even finished saying their goodnights to each other.

In the night, Dylan had a dream. He was looking down from somewhere up high. Below him were the streets of his own neighborhood. People crowded the streets, some wandering slowly, others clipping along at almost a run. Dylan recognized everyone he saw. His teacher was there, his classmates, aunts, uncles, cousins, his doctor, his dentist, people from stores where his family shopped—all people Dylan knew. He could see both of his parents as well. Dylan thought it curious that, even with so many people on the street and all of them known to each other, no one walked with anyone else. Each person walked alone. As he watched, Dylan noticed another strange fact. In spite of the ceaseless activity, no one ever actually got anywhere. People would walk in one direction for a while, then, either turning sharply on their heel or moving around in a great arc, they all ended up going back the way they had come. Later, they would turn again and go the other way once more.

A voice interrupted Dylan's observations, a voice Dylan had come to thoroughly dislike. It belonged to Mr. Smith, the man who kept trying to discourage him and Clare from looking for a real Holiday. "So tell me, Dylan, why do you hate your parents?" the voice asked.

"That's crazy! I don't hate my parents!" Dylan protested.

"Oh, you don't," the voice answered (but Dylan could not see the speaker anywhere). "But you certainly don't think much about what they want, do you? You have this obsession with finding a real Holiday and getting authorized so you can stay there—what does that say to them about how much you appreciate all they've done for you? *Their* house where *they* live isn't good enough for you. You don't appreciate that they've taken you on vacations to Holiday every year; oh, no, you want to find the *real* Holiday, and then you want to stay there forever, even though you know your father needs to stay where he is for his job."

Dylan started to protest, but the voice, going on, cut him short. "Of course, I can see why you might not care much about them. I mean, how much have they cared about you? They know how much you want to live in Holiday; why don't they move there? Could it be that a job and the things they own matter more to them than you do? If there is a real Holiday, and since it's so important to you, why don't they help you get there?" Dylan remembered his parents' encouragement to take as long as he needed to look for the Founder and to try to get authorized. He remembered his father telling him it was the most important trip he would ever make. But the voice went on relentlessly, as if the speaker could read Dylan's mind. "If they think it's so important, why haven't they worked a little harder at trying to get you there?" Then the voice concluded, and the fact that it spoke so pleasantly made the words all the more awful to hear. "No, Dylan, your parents are like you, and you're like everyone else. You're all so wrapped up in your own concerns and interests that you don't have time or energy left to care about what other people might want or need. It's all about 'me first,' for all of you. Want proof? Go see."

Abruptly (as often happens in a dream), Dylan's position changed. No longer did he look down on the scene from above; he himself walked with all the other people on the street. Like everyone else, he walked all alone. Now Dylan noticed what he had not seen before. The people were not only walking; they gestured with their arms at one another and their mouths moved so that it looked like they shouted to one another; yet an eerie silence hung over the street.

Dylan wanted to be with someone he knew, so he looked around for his father. When he caught his eye, he waved and shouted. "Dad! Where are you going?" Dylan distinctly heard his own voice, too loud in the great stillness. His father, however, cupped his hand to his ear to indicate that he had not heard what Dylan had called. Dylan shouted the same thing again, louder, but still his father could not hear him. His father's mouth moved, as though he too shouted at Dylan, but Dylan could hear nothing but his own voice. "Well, I don't care *where* you're going," Dylan muttered, "*I* don't have anywhere I have to go; I'll walk with you." So Dylan tried to move toward his father, only to discover, frighteningly, that his legs would not do what he wanted them to do. Try as he would to change directions, Dylan could not get his legs to do anything other than move straight ahead. He could not turn.

Dylan felt a rising panic. He had never thought much about his legs; they had always done what he wanted them to do without any special attention. It scared him now to have them move as though they had their own lives, outside of his control. Where would they take him? Then he saw his mother, walking quickly. She saw him at the same time, and stretched out her arms to him. At first he thought she would come to him, but then he saw that her course would take her right past him, just out of his reach. Once again, he tried to alter his direction—it would only take the slightest movement!—but still his legs would not obey. Now Dylan understood why all the people walked alone. Each one walked at a slightly different angle, so that no two would ever meet and none had the power to change direction. Nor could anyone hear anything except his or her own voice.

Dylan's father came into view once more. He reached for Dylan, who reached back, but their fingers touched only empty air. In Dylan's dream, he walked for hours, maybe days, in the same relentless, solitary, silent circles. Sometimes, when he could no longer stand the silence, he would try calling out again, but no one could ever hear him. For a while, he talked to himself, just to have something to listen to. His voice sounded so strange in the deafening stillness that he soon gave that up.

At last, in despair, Dylan heard himself say, "I'm going to be all alone forever." Suddenly, he was no longer in the crowd, but watching again from above. Only this time, he could see himself down there, still walking alone. Mr. Smith spoke again. "Don't worry, Dylan," he said, soothingly, "it's just a dream." Then his voice developed an ever-so-slight edge to it. "But it's a dream that shows you what real life is like. In real life, every person cares first of all about his or her own pointless little life. Any interest real people have in each other is only on the surface. It's just to be polite, to mask the fact that all that really matters is what *I'm* doing, what *I* want. People tell each other all their thoughts and feelings, but, in the end, no one really cares. Everyone is too busy thinking about his or her *own* concerns to really listen well to someone else.

"You should have been content with your vacations in Holiday, young man," the voice added. "Everyone's nice to each other while they're there, and all this ugliness doesn't show. If there *is* a real Holiday, *you* can't live there. Neither can anyone else. Remember the first thing on that list? Look out for others' interests, not just your own. Do you see any of that going on down there? Did you see any of that on your way here today? And what about you? What about you and choosing sides for baseball, you and an old man who moves too slowly, you and your parents at church on Sundays? Forget it, young man, there can't be a real Holiday. No one fits the requirements for living there."

When Dylan awoke, he felt like he had never slept. "Good morning," said Clare. "I've been waiting for you to wake up."

Dylan did not respond to Clare's greeting. He merely said, "I'm going home."

"What?" asked Clare. "Why? What about Holiday?"

"There can't be any such place," Dylan said flatly. "There aren't any people who would meet the requirements for living there. And even if there *were* people who met the requirements, I wouldn't be one of them." He pulled the list out of his pocket. He looked it over once more and snorted in disgust at himself. "I don't meet any of these requirements, let alone all of them."

Clare did not know how to answer him. Then Missy's clear, sweet voice chimed in. "I'm not listening in on purpose," she said, "but it's a pretty small park, you know. It's hard *not* to hear everything that's said. I'm not sure you're reading very carefully, young man," she said to Dylan. "Do you see anything on that list in your hand that says a person is required to do all these things before he can be authorized for Holiday?"

"Sure, it says right here," and Dylan read from the paper, "Authorized Personnel will look out for the interests of others, pay back evil for good . . ." and Dylan went on to read the whole list.

When he had finished, Missy asked, "Did you read the whole paper?"

"Yes," Dylan answered.

"Well, I didn't hear anything about requirements for being authorized, did you?"

"Yes," Dylan replied impatiently, "it says 'Authorized Personnel will—"

Missy interrupted. "Don't read it all again. Pay attention to what you're reading. All it says is, 'Authorized Personnel *will*' do those things. The question is: will they do them in order to *become* authorized? Or will they do those things once they *are* authorized?"

Dylan looked again at the paper in his hand and realized she had a point. "Let me tell you a thing or two about the Founder," Missy continued. "He knows what people are like. He knows it much better than people themselves know it.

That's why everyone's first trip to Holiday includes a stroll through those parts of town you passed through yesterday. He wants the travelers themselves to see that there is nothing about them that makes them good candidates for authorization. If anyone ever *is* authorized for Holiday, it's because the Founder is just good enough to authorize them, that's all."

Dylan felt the faintest twinges of renewed hope. "I don't get it," he said. "If that's right, then what's the point of this list at all?"

"For one thing, it's a reminder," Missy explained. "The Emperor does indeed have his list of requirements for what his subjects must do and be. But they've so hopelessly botched things that none of them could ever meet those requirements. The Founder not only paid what they owed the Emperor, he also offered himself to the Emperor as the one who would meet all those requirements for them.

"Then, the list also tells you what authorized personnel *will* be," Missy explained patiently. "The Founder doesn't leave people the way they are; he changes them. There are none who fit that list before he authorizes them, but once they're authorized, they become, little by little, what that list describes. And there you have another good reason why people hang me, Missy Mistletoe, in every part of Holiday! Its authorized personnel were reconciled to their Emperor, *and* they were reconciled to each other."

"So it's really not about me meeting a list of requirements?" Dylan said. (You may think it was taking him a long time to get the point, but the idea was such surprising good news to him that he almost felt he must have misunderstood.)

"No, dear," Missy said with deliberate patience, "it's all about the Founder. Now, you two need to eat some breakfast and get on your way. You have places to go and things to do."

"And people to meet," Dylan added. "Do you think we'll find the Founder soon?" For as much as Dylan wanted to see the real Holiday, and as badly as he needed the Founder's authorization in order to do that, he had begun to want to find the Founder for his own sake, just to meet this wonderful hero who kept showing up in every Holiday story.

"You don't find the Founder; he finds you," Missy answered, in those same words Dylan had heard several times before. "He's not just the Founder; he's the Finder too." Only when Missy said them in her sweet clear voice, they sounded serious and exciting.

"Where should we go?" Clare asked just as Dylan was saying, "What should we do next?"

Missy laughed her tinkling laugh. "Breakfast first," she insisted. "I know it's what your mothers would want. Then, go back out the gate and turn at the corner. You'll find yourself in the Village of Holiday, where the candlemaker has his shop. I'm sure you'll find him more than helpful."

7

Lost in the Dark

lare's anxiety about leaving the park to go back to the streets where ill will flowed so freely proved unfounded. No sooner had she and Dylan turned the corner, as Missy had said, than they found themselves in a picturesque village street. Homey, inviting shops lined the narrow lane. Flowers smiled from window boxes. Delicious odors floated from bakery doors to tickle their noses. "Now we're on the right track," Dylan announced. "This is beginning to be like what we could see of Holiday."

"This must be the outskirts of the city," Clare agreed. "Everything's 'Holiday Village' this or that. There's Holiday Village Flowers, Holiday Village Toys, and, mmm, Holiday Village Bakery." Clare drew in a deep breath filled with the fragrance of baking bread.

"Well, then, Holiday Village Candles must be around here somewhere," Dylan said. They continued past the

Holiday Village Gift Shop, Holiday Village Home Décor, and the Holiday Village Café. Fresh fruit stands, hardware stores, bookstands, and clothing shops—Holiday Village had it all! But where was the candle shop? As the cousins walked down the main street, the shops became fewer and fewer and were finally replaced by farm fields. "We must have missed it," Dylan said, and they returned the way they had come.

"Maybe it's on a side street," Clare suggested.

"Maybe," Dylan replied, "but I thought I looked down every one we passed. They didn't seem to have anything but houses." Dylan lit up. "Maybe that's it. Maybe the candle shop is in someone's house."

The cousins went back and walked up and down each side street. They found nothing but cute little houses in cute little yards—no shops at all. So they walked all the way down the main street again, peering carefully at every sign and into every store window. No candle shop.

"I guess we'll have to ask someone," Clare said.

"There was a stand back there that said 'Visitor's Information,'" Dylan said. Back they went to look. Dylan studied the map posted at the stand. Every shop was listed and numbered in the margin, with the numbers placed on the map. Pointing to the candle shop's number on the map, Dylan said, "That's funny. I'm sure we've been by there, but we didn't see a candle shop. I guess we'll just have to go look again."

One more time, Dylan led the way back. Clare saw Holiday Hats, a shoe store, and a pet shop. No candle store. "Hey! Here's a little sign!" called Dylan, who had been searching carefully. He pointed to a sign in the shape of an arrow. The sign was not as high as Dylan's knee. A bush partially hid it.

"No wonder we missed it!" said Clare. "But what does it mean? I don't see a candle shop that direction either." The sign was on the corner of a street and seemed to be pointing at Holiday Hats on the corner.

"Maybe there's something *behind* Holiday Hats," Dylan suggested. "Maybe that's what it means." He was already moving off around the corner to see. Once around the corner, Dylan and Clare discovered a narrow winding alley. Another small arrow-shaped sign pointed down the alley to "CANDLES."

"Odd place for a candle shop," Clare muttered, following Dylan down the alley and around a turn. That brought them face to face with a brick wall. The alley angled off in another direction. Then it twisted, and turned again. Clare chuckled. "It's better than a maze!" she said.

They continued down the alley, twisting, turning, winding. Each change of direction forced Dylan's eyes to work a little harder to be able to see. After several minutes of increasing darkness, he said, "Why is it so dark?"

"Because it winds around so much," Clare answered. "All the walls block out the light from the street."

"But what about the light from the sky?" Dylan asked. "There wasn't any kind of roof over the alley. There should be light from the sky. It wasn't even noon when we came in, but it's as dark as night in here."

"That's right," said Clare glancing up. "I was thinking we came in under a roof, but we didn't. Why *is* it so dark? I can hardly see."

The two went on in silence for a few minutes. Dylan's head had begun to hurt from staring so intensely into darkness. He had been walking very slowly, to keep from tripping or from bumping into anything, and now he stopped altogether. "I can't see a thing," he confessed.

From what seemed far away, he faintly heard Clare's startled answer. "Dylan, where *are* you?"

"Where are *you?*" he answered, wondering how she could have wandered so far from him in such a narrow alley. In the end, Dylan had to keep calling to Clare while he groped his way through the darkness in the general direction of her answering voice. Even when he had finally drawn close enough to her to touch her, he could not make out her form in the dark.

Clare clutched at Dylan's arm. "I'm scared," she said. "I've never seen darkness like this before, not even in the Cave. You can *feel* this darkness, like it's pressing down on us. It seems like if you stayed in here long enough, it would crush you. I think we should go back."

Dylan shook his head, then realized that was pointless since Clare could not see his head. "No," he said, "it was really scary in the Cave and we wanted to go back, but that turned out okay. It was just part of getting to the Forest of Life. The sign pointed into the alley, so I'm sure we're doing the right thing. All we have to do is get back to the wall, then feel our way along it to the end of the alley—and the candle shop." Abruptly, Dylan returned to the subject that was puzzling him. "Clare, how did we get so far apart when this alley is so narrow? Anyway, it *was* narrow. . . ." His voice trailed off into a puzzled, unspoken question as he inched his way forward, one arm outstretched (Clare held on to his other one), feeling for the wall. His hand met nothing but empty darkness.

"Here," Dylan said, "hold my hand instead. Use your other hand to feel for the wall. It's got to be right here somewhere!"

Dylan and Clare moved in ever widening circles, both of them feeling all around them for the wall. Five minutes passed, ten, maybe fifteen—no wall yet. "This is *crazy*," Dylan mumbled. "It was just an alley. There were buildings on both sides. And it was morning on a sunny day. Now the walls are gone, we're in a wide open space, and it's pitch dark." He was silent for a moment. Then Clare felt his fingers go cold, and he asked, "Clare, which direction were we going?"

"I don't know," Clare replied in a voice so small that it did indeed sound as if the darkness had crushed it.

Without a word, Dylan and Clare began to walk again. They felt that they could not just sit there in the darkness. Trying to get *somewhere* was better than doing nothing. So they walked, feeling their way with their hands in front of them, the way blind people might. Before each step, they felt the ground in front of them with their feet to be sure of it. The cousins might as well have had no eyes at all, for all the use they were. Even as a small child, Dylan had never been afraid of the dark. But Clare was right; this was a different darkness than any he had ever known before. It seemed to have a life of its own. Dylan felt that the darkness knew they were there and that it did not wish them well. Just as cold has a way of creeping into your bones, so it seemed to Dylan that this darkness wanted to get inside of him, to be a part of him—or to absorb him into itself.

The cousins had inched along in the crushing darkness for what felt like hours when Dylan noticed that his eyes had begun to play tricks on him. He could see what appeared to be a tiny pinprick of red light. Even though he realized that this was just one of those spots your eyes see sometimes when they're closed or when it's very dark, he stared at the tiny red dot. At least it was something to look at. Suddenly, he felt Clare's hand tighten in his own. "Dylan! There's a light!" she whispered in excitement. "Or something."

"Or something" was right. The children had quickened their pace. As they approached the light, however, they saw not exactly a light, but a patch of deep red color, faintly glow-ing. Without saying anything to each other, both Dylan and Clare slowed their steps. Somehow, the red glow did not seem much friendlier than the intense dark. Soon the children could see that the glow came from a torch held in someone's hand. Their hearts sank when they recognized the torchbearer. It was Mr. Smith. Nei-ther of them trusted his pleasant face or his smooth voice any longer.

"Oh, my, look who's here," he said now, as though he were surprised to see them. Dylan and Clare both felt sure he had been looking for them. "This darkness is much too dangerous for you to be wan-dering about in," he continued. "Were you looking for something?"

"We were looking for the wall," Dylan answered, coldly. As he spoke, he looked around by the torch's glow. There was no wall to be seen.

"Well," the man smiled agreeably, "of course you didn't come in here in the first place to find a wall. What were you looking for when you came in?"

"The candle shop," Clare replied.

"Wanted some light, did you? Well, this is your lucky day. I'm going to show you that life in here, yes, in this very darkness, can be so glorious, you'll never want another candle. If you'll follow me, I'll lead you to some folks who will show you what I mean."

"I don't trust him," Clare whispered to Dylan.

"I know, but what choice do we have? Maybe the people he's talking about will know how to get to the candle shop. Let's just go see," Dylan whispered back.

So the children set off in the eerie glow of Mr. Smith's torch. As they walked, he chattered good-naturedly. "I think you'll like the D Der's," he began. "That's what I call the people I'm going to introduce you to. They're very sensible. You'll like that about them. They're able to look at things realistically, and then choose the best course. And they're always happy. The D Der's know how to enjoy life. They don't miss a thing!"

As he chattered on, Dylan and Clare became aware of noise up ahead. It sounded like a party. They heard voices, music, and laughter. The closer they got to the noise, however, the less they liked it, and their initial relief at hearing human voices faded. Dylan and Clare realized that while many of the voices laughed, others cursed. The laughter itself, lacking any note of joy, contained a mocking, jeering ring. The music had a sinister pulse to it. Dylan felt Clare tug at his hand. He stopped.

"Hold it," Dylan said. Mr. Smith stopped. Maybe it was a shadow from the flicker of the torch, or maybe a trace of impatience flitted across his face. He still sounded pleasant, though, as he said, "What is it?"

"Who did you say these people are?" Dylan asked.

The man chuckled. "Oh, I just said I call them D Der's. Those are just initials, you know."

"Well, what do they stand for?" Dylan wanted to know.

"Darkness Dwellers." The man said it quickly, and hurried on. "They are so good at making the best of things, you can't imagine. They've made such a nice place—a nice *real* place, not like a pretend Holiday. They have so much fun! They enjoy every possible pleasure. You can't help but enjoy life with the D Der's. They'll show you how to have a good time—a great time, every day. You'll never—"

"Darkness Dwellers?" Dylan interrupted. "You mean these people live here in this darkness?"

"Oh, yes," Mr. Smith nodded pleasantly. "And it's a wonderful thing. They're smart enough to realize what would happen if they ever got out into the light. But it's not like you think.

They have their own lights that they've made for themselves, like mine here," and he waved his torch. "The D Der's have every comfort, every happiness."

"What *would* happen if they went out into the light?" Clare asked.

"Why, everyone would see what they're doing. That wouldn't be good," and the man shook his head.

"What *are* they doing?" asked Dylan.

"Ah-ah." Mr. Smith waved his finger at Dylan. "That would be telling. You'll find out soon enough. Just trust me; I promise you'll like it just as much as they do."

"I don't think so," Dylan said, just as Clare was saying, "Dylan, I don't want to go with him."

"What? You want to keep looking *in here*—" and Mr. Smith gestured widely with his torch—"for candles?" And it did sound ridiculous when he said it. "You'll never get out of this darkness, you know. That's the whole point of darkness. You can't see in it. You can't find anything. You can't tell where you're going. You've only been here a very little while—what will you be like days from now? Think about that." (Both children *had* been thinking about that, and they did not at all care for the thought.) "You'd be much better off learning from the D Der's how you can make a home, a wonderful home, right here—without candles."

"My idea of a wonderful home is not living in pitch darkness for the rest of my life," Dylan answered firmly. "Not even with a bunch of your weird little red lights. I'm sure there's a way out" (but he wasn't), "and we're going to find it."

"Suit yourselves," the man snapped, not at all pleasantly this time. He turned on his heel and strode off, the darkness growing deeper and heavier by degrees as the red glow went away with him.

When it had finally disappeared altogether, Clare said to Dylan, "Are you really sure there's a way out?"

Dylan was not at all sure of any such thing, but he wanted to encourage Clare. "There's got to be a way out," he replied. "The cave seemed every bit as hopeless as this does, and we got out of there."

"Right," Clare agreed. "You have no more idea of the way out than I do. But I'm glad you said we wouldn't go see the D Der's. That can't be the solution! Listen to them."

The children listened to the distant shouts. For all that their guide had insisted that the Darkness Dwellers were happy, and for all that the children still heard laughter, something in the laughter sounded strained, distressed even. "I wonder what they *are* doing that they don't want anyone to see," Dylan muttered.

"Let's go," was Clare's only reply.

Refusing the pleasant-faced Mr. Smith and avoiding the D Der's had given Dylan and Clare a new burst of energy. Resisting the easy way had made them feel brave, and they moved off into the darkness with fresh hope. All too soon, however, the darkness resumed its steady pressure, and they felt their hope shrinking. At last it began to seem to Dylan that he had been walking in darkness all his life. His weary legs stumbled with every other step, and his eyes burned with strain because they would not stop trying to see in the dark. *And who knows if we're even going in the right direction,* he thought.

Just then Clare said, "Dylan, I've had it. I can't walk anymore."

"Yeah," Dylan said flatly, stopping. The two sank to the ground. There was nothing to lean on, since they had never found the wall, so Dylan stretched out on the ground. Clare did too, saying, "What if someone comes through here? They'll never see us, and they'll walk right over the top of us."

Dylan meant to answer, but went to sleep before he could.

Dylan and Clare awoke at the same time. They had no way to know how long they had slept or whether it was night or day. The darkness had not changed. They sat up and rummaged in their bag for something to eat, which they ate listlessly, with no appetite. "I guess we might as well walk a while?" Clare suggested.

Dylan thought *Why? What's the point?* but he didn't say it. He just rose wearily to his feet and reached for Clare's hand. Far, far in the distance, he thought he saw, just for an instant, a quick, small flash. He stared, but it did not reappear. *Just my imagination,* he thought. *Of course.* He sighed. But there it flashed again—maybe. He peered ahead, waiting, and saw a longer flash. "Clare," he said cautiously. "Do you see anything? Besides darkness, I mean."

"You mean like some quick flashes?" she answered. "I was afraid I was seeing things." The two watched as the flashes came more and more often and grew larger and longer. Soon, the flashes had become a steady light, small, but clearly coming in their direction.

"What if it's *him* again?" Clare asked. "Will we go with him?"

Dylan thought with distaste of the eerie red glow, the nasty little man who only seemed pleasant, and the evil sounds of the Darkness Dwellers. But then he thought of the steady, crushing, unrelenting darkness and wondered how long he could bear it. Clare was waiting for an answer. "I don't know," Dylan said simply.

8

The Candlemaker

T he new light in the darkness had nothing eerie about it. It beamed bright, white, and cheerful. It merely had to appear for Dylan and Clare to feel their despair and confusion melt away. As it drew closer, the children saw that it came from a tall candlestick, held high. Wondering at a mere candle this bright, Clare saw, on the right and on the left, the walls of the alley they had felt for so unsuccessfully. The alley extended just a little farther, then came to a dead end at the back door of a shop. In the window, a sign read, "HOLIDAY VILLAGE CANDLES."

The children stared at the man who carried the candle and who walked briskly toward them. A stiff white apron covered his clothes, almost to his ankles, but it did not slow him in the least. By the candle's clear light, splatters, in a rainbow of colors, stood out all over the apron. Its two large pockets had been crammed full of candles. Dylan and Clare saw the ends peeking out. From the man's shirt pocket, where usually pens would appear, more candles peeked out. When the man reached the children, he stopped, looking down at them with a serious expression. But behind his spectacles, his dark eyes twinkled.

"You must be the candlemaker," Dylan said.

With his free hand, the man patted a candle-stuffed apron pocket. "Good guess," he said, the slightest hint of a smile playing around one corner of his mouth. "Were you looking for my shop?" Dylan and Clare nodded eagerly. "This way, then," he said, turning toward the door they saw just ahead. "It's right here."

"Then we were almost there!" Dylan said.

The candlemaker stood still and turned his head to peer at Dylan over the tops of his spectacles. "Of course you weren't," he replied. "You would never have found the way by yourself." Dylan opened his mouth to ask a question, but the man had started off again and, in spite of his snow-white hair, he walked so quickly that Dylan and Clare had to hurry to keep up. Together they entered the back door of Holiday Village Candles.

The candlemaker set his tall candle down on the counter and blew it out, since there was no need for it inside. The shop's many windows all stood open. Through them, Clare saw the garden that surrounded the little store on three sides. Sunlight streamed in at these windows and, outside, birds twittered and sang. A calendar hung on the wall. Glancing at it and at the clock near it, Dylan, amazed, realized that it was

still morning on the same day they had entered the dark alley. It had *felt* like a lifetime of darkness! Then he saw an open door leading out into the garden. Clare had already walked through it, and Dylan followed. A bench sat squarely in the center of the yard where no shade reached. Gratefully, Dylan and Clare sank down onto this bench and turned their faces, eyes closed, up to the sunlight.

Dylan and Clare took their time soaking up light. When they finally reentered the shop, the candlemaker was busy in back, in the work area. The smell of melting wax reached the children as they surveyed the contents of the shop. "Who ever would have thought there could be so many different kinds of candles?" Clare murmured.

Shelves lined the walls between the windows. Candles of all varieties filled every inch of every shelf. Long tall tapers and round little candles that were almost balls, thick sturdy candles and tiny little delicate ones, plain white candles and candles in every bright or pastel color imaginable—the shelves held all these. Out on the floor, tables and racks that turned held more candles. Some had been carved into exquisite forms, and some even into tiny scenes. Dylan and Clare kept busy for some time, calling back and forth, "Hey, look at this one!" and "Come see this!" At some point, Clare realized the candle-maker was leaning in the doorway between his shop and his work area, watching them. "These are wonderful candles," she said to him.

Once again, he almost smiled as he said, "Want one? You may choose one for free, you know. Any one you like."

"Thanks!" the children said, and went back to looking at candles with renewed interest since now they each needed to make a choice. Clare chose a little wax scene with a wick, but, of course, she had no intention of ever lighting it. It was too pretty for that. Dylan chose a tall elegant taper. He thought his mother might like it. They brought their choices to the candlemaker, who wrapped them carefully in boxes, to prevent their being broken in Dylan's pack.

Once Dylan had safely arranged the candles in the pack, the candlemaker said, "That's that! Anything else I can do for you?"

"Well," Dylan answered, "we were wondering what you could tell us about the Founder. That's really who we're looking for, and Missy Mistletoe, back at the park, told us you might be able to help us."

"The Founder, is it?" said the candlemaker. "For one thing, I work for the Founder. He's the one who called me to work here, making candles. I've been doing it for years."

"Did you build this shop?" Clare asked.

"Oh, no, it's much older than I am," the candlemaker replied. "Holiday Village Candles was one of the first stores in Holiday. As soon as building began on the ruins of the old city the tyrants had ruled, the Founder insisted that there be a candle shop, because people must have light. Holiday is full of light now—all kinds of lights, not just candles. Surely you've seen them? Little white lights, bright colorful lights, strings of lights, all kinds. And there are still plenty of candles. But the candles came first, from right here in this shop."

"Why not put some lights in that alley?" Dylan asked. "This shop's almost impossible to get to!"

Frowning slightly, the candlemaker stared Dylan full in the face. "What do you mean 'almost?'" he said. "I tell you, you would never have found the way by yourself. The alley is left over from the rule of the tyrants. Before, when the tyrants reigned, the darkness covered the whole city." Clare shuddered. "The tyrants liked it that way. It kept their subjects from escaping. How could they get away when they couldn't even see where they were going? When the Founder chased out the tyrants, he chased out the darkness as well—except in that alley. But it won't last forever. There are plans to demolish it one of these days."

"But meantime, the only way to your shop is through the alley," Dylan said. "That seems awfully dangerous."

The candlemaker almost smiled. "Not to worry," he said. "The Founder's very careful about not losing anyone. That's why he sends me out with my candle several times every day, looking for people just like you who are on the way to the candle shop. It's part of my job."

"But what if you miss someone?" Dylan wanted to know. "It's awfully dark out there, and it really *is* big, isn't it? Or did it just *seem* big?" Dylan glanced at the door leading to the alley, but it shut out the darkness, and he could see no trace of it.

"Oh, that darkness is much greater than you could ever imagine," the candlemaker assured him. "But I've never missed anyone who was supposed to get to my shop. Never." He shook his head with certainty. "It's not possible."

"But we heard other people out there," Clare protested. "Why haven't you led *them* out?"

"You mean the D Der's—the Darkness Dwellers?" the candlemaker asked. Both children nodded. "I've invited them plenty of times," he said. "But they never want to come."

"How did they start living there in the first place?" Dylan asked.

"They're left from when the tyrants ruled," the candlemaker said. "They settled in there back then, and they never wanted anything different. When the new Ruler came and drove out the tyrants, they actually resented it! They liked things the way they had always been. So there they stayed. Later generations were born there, in the darkness, and they all liked it too. So I go in sometimes, but I only make them angry. They don't want light."

"That's crazy," said Clare, shaking her head. "Why would they prefer that hideous darkness to light?"

"They don't want anyone to see what they're doing," the candlemaker answered. "If they came out into the light, everyone would see."

"What *are* they doing?" Clare asked.

A brief shudder flitted across the strong features of the candlemaker's face. "I don't want to talk about it," he answered, "and, trust me, you don't want to know."

"Say!" A new idea had struck Dylan. "You said the Founder sends you out to find people who are looking for your shop, and you said that you never miss anyone who's supposed to find it. That almost sounds like—" Dylan hesitated, reluctant to speak his thought out loud.

"Yes?" the candlemaker folded his arms and tapped his foot with a trace of impatience. "Go on. Say it."

"Well, it sounds like—like maybe the Founder knew we were coming," Dylan said.

With a nod, the candlemaker answered, "Of course he did. And?"

Encouraged, Dylan continued. "And maybe he knows we're trying to get into the real Holiday and get authorized so we can come and go whenever we want."

"Young man, that should be obvious to you by now," the candlemaker replied. "How do you think you got this far? I mean, I'm guessing you got stuck in a cave, but a voice called you out and you ended up in Life Forest. Right?" Dylan nodded. "And I'll just bet, somewhere along the way, you realized you'd lost your visitor's pass, but when you got to the park, you learned your fine was paid in full and another pass was waiting. Am I right?"

Dylan nodded again. "But how did you know?" he asked. The candlemaker chuckled ever so briefly and ever so quietly. "Oh, it just comes with working here for so many years. There's a kind of pattern I often see."

Even more encouraged, Dylan went on. "Well, if the Founder knows we're trying to get authorized and if he's been sort of working things out to help us, well, he probably *will* authorize us, won't he? And where can we find him? I'd really like to meet him."

The candlemaker's eyes twinkled. "You know what I'm going to say next, don't you?" Dylan's face fell as the candlemaker began, "You don't find the Founder, he finds you—" Dylan sighed and finished along with the candlemaker, "He's not just the Founder; he's the Finder too." There was a brief pause, then, still in unison, they said, "That rhymed."

The candlemaker chuckled. "You're getting it," he said. "But don't be discouraged. And you're right—there's nothing more important than finding the Founder. So let me tell you what to try next. Surely you've noticed that, in between Holiday Village here and the real Holiday proper, there's an odd-shaped mountain, not very wide but very tall. It really just goes straight up then straight down again. You've noticed that, right?" The children nodded. "Have you seen the little building at the top?" Neither of the children had. "Not surprising," the candlemaker continued. "It's a pretty small building. Well, the building is a little church—very, very old. It has bells up in the tower. Those bells can tell you about the Founder. I suggest you go talk to them."

"We don't have to go back the same way—through that darkness—do we?" Clare asked.

"Oh, no," the candlemaker shook his head. "Just go on out into the garden and through the gate. Follow the street to the right and just keep going. You can't miss it, because you'll always see the mountain in front of you. And the church is the only building on it. But," he added, "if it's an easy stroll you're wanting, this isn't it. That mountain's high and steep; only serious hikers get to the top."

"But it can be climbed, right?" Dylan double-checked.

The candlemaker nodded. "It can be climbed," he assured them, "as long as you really want to climb it."

The two cousins thanked the candlemaker for his help, for the candles, and for his advice. Then they were out the door, through the garden, and heading off down the street.

As soon as Dylan and Clare stepped out from behind the trees surrounding the candle shop, they saw the mountain, rising tall in front of them. There was something almost comical about its appearance, as it shot straight up into the air, like an upside down ice cream cone. *There won't be anything funny about trying to get up that, though,* Dylan thought. *That's steep!*

"Well," Clare said, almost as if she had heard Dylan's thoughts, "this part of our hike is nice enough. It's an easy road, the weather's perfect—not a cloud in the sky. And isn't *that* great after that dark alley?"

They had come to the very edge of Holiday Village. There were hardly any shops here, and even the houses grew scarce, with great stretches of open field between them. The road itself remained fairly level, in spite of the great mountain waiting at the end of it. Clearly, this road's only purpose was to lead hikers to the mountain. It did not skirt around the bottom or branch off in some other direction. It marched straight up to the mountain, then stopped. At least, that was how it appeared until Dylan and Clare actually stood at the mountain's base. There they found the road, transformed into a narrow footpath, going on and up. "Oh, good," Dylan said, "at least there's a trail," and up they started.

From the very beginning, the trail proved to be much harder even than it had looked. For one thing, it was terribly steep. (Clare did not like to think about going back down. What would keep you from running or sliding all the way?) Every few minutes, both children had to stop to get their breath, and muscles in their legs protested the unaccustomed strain. Sometimes, the trail would disappear under a pile of rocks, and the hikers would have to clamber up and over huge boulders the best they could until the trail appeared again on the other side. Other times, the trail crossed great flat surfaces of slanted, slippery stone or flows of small, loose rocks that could easily shift. Dylan would glance down and wonder briefly what would happen if the rocks began to move under his feet.

All the while, the trail continued to wind around and around the mountain, always leading higher. The road down at the bottom appeared first as a wide scarf, later as a slender belt, and finally as the thinnest of ribbons. At that point, Holiday Village itself, and Holiday, right next to it, were tiny toy towns alone in a great valley. "Let's take a break," Clare panted, and Dylan nodded, out of breath himself. They went far enough from the path to get under the scant shade of a large boulder and sat down.

"It's *hot!*" Dylan said, holding his sweaty shirt out away from his skin, hoping to catch any breeze that might happen by. None did.

"I need some water," Clare said, reaching to open the backpack Dylan carried.

Dylan stiffened. "Oh no," he groaned, "I forgot to fill the bottle back at the candle shop. I don't think there's much left."

Clare pulled out the bottle. Dylan was right. Only a few mouthfuls remained in the bottom. "Of course, I didn't feel all that thirsty before," Dylan said, "but now I do."

They each drank a swallow, leaving the tiniest bit more for one last drink. Once they had caught their breath, they began the climb anew. Of course, the closer to the top they climbed, the harder it grew. The path became ever steeper, the sun beat ever hotter, their clothing became ever wetter with perspiration, and their legs began to tremble. And still they had more trail ahead—the hardest part of it at that.

The cousins paused to rest again, but this time there was nothing big enough to give shade anywhere near. They stood on the trail with the hot sun beating down on them and warming the air they were gasping. "Do you think this is worth it?" Dylan said, more to himself than to Clare. "To talk to some bells? There must be plenty of other people in Holiday that could tell us about the Founder."

"Well," Clare said, almost reluctantly. (The thought of stopping *was* attractive.) "The candlemaker said we should do this. And remember, he said it's possible to get to the top; you just have to really want it."

"That's just it," Dylan answered. "I'm beginning to wonder if I want it this much," but he started back up the path again. After going only a few more steps, Dylan suddenly stopped. Clare, who had been watching her feet on the trail, almost bumped into him. Startled, she looked up to see why he had stopped.

The children had rounded a corner. There, right in front of them, just at the very edge of the trail, stood a tree, the only one they had seen on their hike. It was not a large tree, but it was taller than a person and its branches reached out and provided shade. Under the tree, taking up every inch of the shadow it threw, stood a wooden booth, painted bright blue. On either side of the booth, a canvas chair, well-shaded, hung from the tree. Over the booth, a banner read, "R&R REST AND REFRESHMENT" and underneath it, in smaller letters, "SEEKING? COME IN HERE." On the counter, tall glasses waited next to pitchers of iced liquids.

The first reaction of both of the cousins was relief. They could taste, they could feel, the icy liquids going down their throats. But they had not been imagining this for even one full moment when they saw the problem. They knew the man who sat behind the counter. It was Mr. Smith. "Welcome, welcome," he called out, beaming. "Don't *you* look like you could use a break?"

9

The Bell Choir

e'd love a break, and a drink especially," Dylan answered Mr. Smith, eying the sweating pitchers with longing. "But what's the catch? We know there's a catch."

"No catch, no catch," Mr. Smith replied. "Just come on up, sit down, settle in, stay as long as you like. We'll meet your needs, and we'll make no demands."

"No demands?" Dylan asked with suspicion, reaching for a glass in spite of himself.

"We just want you to be comfortable," the man assured them. He took a pitcher to pour water into the glass Dylan held. "You can stay here forever if you want and we won't ask anything of you. Or you can go back down." The pitcher was over Dylan's glass and the first drop of cool water hung from its lip, ready to fall.

"And up?" Dylan asked. "We can keep going up when we're ready, too, right?"

Mr. Smith straightened the pitcher and jerked it away from the glass Dylan held. "Not up," he said. "This R&R is intended for those who want to stay put or for those going down. Only."

"That's mean!" Clare cried, since Dylan was so startled by the sudden disappointment that he was speechless.

"Me, mean?" the little man protested. "Whoever told you to go up this mountain was mean! I'm offering you shade, rest, refreshments; I'm not mean. What do you think you'll find when you get up there? Some bells, that's all. And what are they going to do? Ring, if anything. How is that worth such a tough climb on such a hot day? You can stay right here and have all you need.

"Not to mention," Mr. Smith continued, reaching down under the counter of his booth, "if it's music you want, check this out." He pulled up a small loudspeaker and set it on the counter. "We have songs about the Founder right here. You don't need to go all the way up there for bells. I promise you'll like these songs—all about the Founder and how good he makes you feel and how much you want to find him. And all the while, you can be sitting right here in a comfortable, shaded chair—"and he gestured at the swinging chairs—"sipping on your favorite beverage."

Dylan, angry in his disappointment over the drink, muttered, "You're pitiful." He turned to Clare. "Come on, Clare, let's go," he said and started on his way again. Clare followed. Behind them, they heard the clinking of ice cubes as Mr. Smith poured a drink. They heard a noisy slurp, followed by a long "aaahh" of satisfaction. A switch clicked and music began to play.

Dylan said nothing. He fixed his eyes on the steep incline ahead. Crunching the gravel underfoot, his feet marched up the trail, his legs moving up, down, up, down in a steady rhythm. Clare found it difficult to keep up. Dylan was angry. She was sure of that, but she was glad to see the difference his anger made in his approach to this last stretch of the trail. It seemed she had left behind at the blue booth a weary, wilting cousin, ready to give up. In his place, a determined hiker now led the way.

Still winding its way around and around to the top, the trail turned another corner. From here, the music from the radio no longer reached them. Clare, who had fallen farther and farther behind, finally called out, "Dylan! Wait for me!" Dylan stopped and waited for Clare to catch up. They both stood and panted.

"Sorry," Dylan said. "Guess I was mad. I am *so* tired of that guy!"

"That's okay," Clare said. "It sure gave you fresh energy!"

"You know," Dylan said, "I don't know why it's so important to that man to keep us from finding the Founder and getting authorized for Holiday, but I do know this. The more he tries to stop us, the more determined I am that it must be worth whatever it takes." Dylan pointed ahead, up the trail. "Look, I think we're almost there. I bet that corner up there is the last one, and the trail after it goes straight to the top. One more big push and we're there."

So they pushed on, and a very big push it proved to be. The trail leading to that last curve in the road was so steep that Clare felt she was walking straight up. Once she rounded the curve, she realized though, that, no, *that* hadn't been straight up; *this* was. A solid wall of rock, several feet taller than her head, met her. She might have thought it impassible, if it weren't that Dylan had already started up. That's when she saw the small foot and handholds scattered about on the rock face. "Here goes nothing," she muttered, and started up after Dylan. She climbed up cautiously, and when she had used the last crack for placing a hand, she found Dylan's hand, reaching down from the top, to help her. Clare took it, scrambled up after him, and stood panting, knees and arms trembling.

Here at the top, a delicious breeze played with their hair and tugged at their clothing. Dylan and Clare turned to face it, letting it dry their perspiration. The top of the mountain was about the size of a small yard for a house. The cousins were surprised to see that it was covered with a lush green lawn. (*I wonder who waters it,* Dylan thought, *and* how *he waters it.*) At the opposite side of the lawn stood the little church, its white, wooden walls weathered, but in good repair. A bell tower rose up from its rear wall. Through the open front door, a shady interior invited entrance.

"I hope there's some water in there," Clare said.

"Let's go see," said Dylan.

They crossed the lawn in a few strides and stepped through the door, finally finding relief from the merciless sun. The church's windows were open and the same delicious breeze they had enjoyed outside blew through the interior. Nothing other than windows decorated the wooden walls. A few roughly fashioned benches sat on the bare concrete floor. Off to the side, a doorway opened onto stairs leading to the bell tower. But the thing that first caught the cousins' attention was the drinking fountain sitting in the back corner of the room. Its cooling unit hummed happily.

"Oh, *yes*," Clare breathed with relief, and hurried across for a drink. She was very thirsty, so while Dylan waited for his turn, he had time to wonder how a drinking fountain could be in such a remote spot—and with an electric cooling unit, even!

When Clare had finished and Dylan stepped up for his drink, he saw a small plaque on the side of the fountain. It read, "Courtesy of the Founder." *Of course*, Dylan thought, *I should have known*. He bent his head and drank what was surely the coolest, freshest water he had ever tasted. Whatever the man at the blue booth had been giving away, it could not have been as good as this.

When Dylan had drunk all he wanted, he straightened to find Clare already through the door leading to the bell tower, her foot poised on the first step. He crossed the room to her, and, Clare in the lead, they climbed up the stairs. The stairs wound round and round, up the tower, and came out on a wooden platform at the very top. The walls here were broken up by large openings, windows with no glass in them. The breeze that had blown gently through the church downstairs, gusted through these windows, causing some swaying among the bells that hung in two rows from beams in the very top of the peaked tower. On one end of each row hung the largest bells. The bells grew progressively smaller down the rows until, at the opposite ends, hung the smallest ones.

The middle-sized bell right in the middle of the front row swayed more than any of the others, so that a slight ringing was actually coming from it. Dylan thought that was strange. He was about to say, "I thought bells were rung by people who pulled ropes," but as he opened his mouth to say it, Clare held up her hand for silence, with a listening expression on

her face. Dylan closed his mouth again and listened. Then he heard it too. The bell was actually ringing words. "All right, everyone," it was saying. "When the wind picks up again, we'll take it from the top, all together this time. Do just like we did it when we rehearsed in sections, and it will be perfect. And altos, remember, stay with the basses, and don't let the tenors get drowned out."

The wind had actually subsided, though, so this little speech was followed by an expectant silence. After several minutes of it, Dylan ventured to say, "Excuse me—uh," (*what* do *you call a talking bell?* he wondered), "Mr.—Conductor?"

This seemed to suit the talking bell just fine, because he immediately responded. "Yes?"

"I don't want to interrupt your rehearsal or anything—" Dylan began.

"Don't worry," the bell interrupted, matter-of-factly. "I won't let you. When the wind picks up, no matter what we're talking about, I will ignore you and we will rehearse. There's so much left to practice, and we must take advantage of every minute."

Dylan hesitated. "But go on," the bell said. "The wind's not blowing hard enough right now, so talk away. Just don't be offended when I cut you off."

"Well," Dylan said quickly, "it was the candlemaker who sent us up here. He said you could tell us more about the Founder of Holiday. See, I've been looking for the Founder so I could get authorized to go into Holiday and to come back whenever I want, and I would still like to do that. But the more I learn about the Founder, the more I think I'd like to get to know him—just to get to know him. So—*are* you able to tell us about the Founder?"

"My dear young man," the bell replied, "that's what we do. That's why we ring. We are the Holiday music and all our music is about the Founder. Have you not noticed the music when you take your Holiday vacations?"

Dylan remembered attending church with his parents when they vacationed in what he had thought was the real Holiday. He remembered how heartily everyone sang then, not like normal times at home. He remembered how he had thought that there must be something special about Holiday music.

"Yes," Dylan said, out loud. "I *have* noticed, and I've wondered why it doesn't last when the vacation's over."

"Because, of course," the bell replied, "most of the people are just that—they're vacationers. They're not authorized and they haven't met the Founder. Since true Holiday music is all about the Founder, how can they keep on singing it with any kind of feeling if they don't know him?"

Dylan would have said something in reply, but, suddenly, the bell said, "Excuse me, young man," and called out, "All right, everyone, on three!" It was then that Dylan noticed that the wind had picked up. If he had not been engaged in the unusual activity of speaking with a bell, he would certainly have noticed the wind, because it blew so hard that he had to brace himself to keep from being pushed backward by it. The bells began to ring. They rang in concert, each ringing its own individual part, but all together creating a true melody, like a choir. They rang gently at first, and over the top of their song the children could hear the voice of the conductor bell. "Right *here* sopranos, stronger, stronger, now smoothly—laaa-tum-tum-tum-dum-de-daaa-dum-de-da." As the wind blew more and more forcefully, the voices of the bells rose in crescendo.

Then the wind gradually subsided, and the song grew softer, softer, and whispered to a close.

All was still. Dylan and Clare felt the need to show their appreciation, but applause did not seem quite appropriate. "That was beautiful," Clare said softly, her eyes shining, just as Dylan said, "Wow! Very nice."

"Hm. Yes, well," the conductor bell began, sounding unconvinced, "it was better. But we still have work to do. Altos, what did I tell you about staying *with* the basses? You can't go running ahead like that or it just won't work!"

Suddenly, a tiny little jingle bell, dislodged by one of the great gusts of wind, fell onto the floor from the window ledge. It hit with a small bounce, then rolled across the floor, jingling all the way. The middle bell sighed an exasperated, "Oh!" and Clare was certain that a suppressed giggle ran through the rows of other bells. "Young man," the middle bell said to Dylan, "would you please pick up that disgusting thing and throw it out the window? I don't know why Holiday visitors insist on bringing those silly, tinny-sounding things up here. They are just *not* music!" Dylan had stopped to pick up the jingle bell. He held it in his hand, looking down at it. "Young man, please," the conductor bell said firmly, "out the window." Dylan shrugged and obeyed. He tossed the jingle bell out the window.

"Thank you," said the middle bell, and his voice sounded friendlier than it had up until now. "What were we saying? Oh, yes, music and the Founder—it's all about him, you know. That's why there's so much of it in Holiday, and that's why it doesn't last when vacationers leave. If they don't really know him, what reason would they have for making music?"

"I know what you're going to say," Dylan began cautiously, "but—you wouldn't know where I could find the Founder, would you?"

The bell's only answer was to hum for pitch. The wind, back up again although not as forcefully, caught the bells and they sang together softly, "You don't find the Founder, he finds you; he's not just the Founder, he's the Finder too." When the short song had ended, the bell added, "But here's what you *can* do. Spend the night up here on the mountaintop. The grass outside is very soft and comfortable, and you'll find some provisions and some blankets in the closet downstairs, left by the Founder, of course." (*Of course*, Dylan thought.) "The stars come down so much closer to this mountaintop than they do anywhere else. They know about the Founder. I don't know that they'd be willing to speak with you. But if they would, you'd be able to hear them here better than anywhere else. Oops, got to go. Here comes the wind again. Everyone, from the top of the page."

What page? Dylan wondered. Then Clare tugged at his sleeve, and he saw that she was moving down into a sitting position on the floor, so the walls would protect her from the wind. He sat down with her, their backs against the wall, and they listened to the wonderful music of the bells.

Dylan and Clare remained in the bell tower listening to the snatches of song that came and went as the wind rose and fell. Occasionally, when the wind subsided, they would stand up and move around the wooden platform to stretch their legs. Finally, as the shadows lengthened and the wind blew more chill, they went back down the bell tower stairs.

"I'm really hungry!" Dylan observed. "It seems like ages since we last ate—when was that, anyway?"

Clare thought. So much had happened. "It must have been in the alley, on the way to the candlemaker's shop," she answered. "That was a while ago! I'm hungry too. I wonder what's in that closet the bell mentioned."

They hurried to the back of the church and opened the closet door. The fragrance of fresh baked bread floated out. A basket of golden crusted rolls, their tops shiny with a thin coating of butter, sat on a small table. "Those *look* good," Dylan said, "but they've got to be hard as rocks. Who knows how long they've been there. And they're not even wrapped in anything."

"Don't be silly," Clare replied. "Smell that! Stale bread doesn't smell like that." And she reached out and took a roll. "It's still warm!" she announced. "These rolls are fresh out of the oven!"

"Well, then that means . . . " Dylan began, and stopped, looking all around as if he expected to see the provider of the bread nearby. No one could possibly hide in the church, tiny as it was, and the cousins could see the entire mountaintop from the window. With no explanation, Dylan bolted to the door and dashed across the grass on the top of the mountain and over to the place where they had come up on the trail. He leaned over the edge, searching the mountainside with his eyes. Clare could see that he did not find what he wanted because, after a moment, he straightened and walked slowly back to the church. He kept looking all around as he walked. Dylan reentered the church. "The bell said the food is provided by the Founder," he explained. "Which doesn't necessarily mean he brought it himself, but *someone* had to bring it. And it must have been in the last few minutes, if the bread's still warm. How can that be? Wouldn't we have seen someone?"

Clare swallowed the piece of bread she was chewing. While waiting for Dylan, she had eaten half the roll she held. "Seems like it," she agreed. "But there's nowhere to hide up here. The more we learn about the Founder, the more amazing he sounds. But I thought you were so hungry—have a roll while they're still hot."

Dylan took a roll and absentmindedly bit it. The roll's flavor startled him, and for a moment he forgot the puzzle of where the bread had come from and studied the roll itself. "That *is* good," he agreed. "That may be the best bread I've ever tasted," and he took another bite. "The Founder obviously knows we're here and he obviously knows we're trying to find him. It's almost like he's following us!"

Clare shook her head firmly. "No, it's not like he's following us. He's going *ahead* of us. We're following him. Think about it," she continued. "You said his voice called you out of the cave, and it was actually *your* name he called. Then, when we got to the park where Missy Mistletoe lives, and you'd lost your visitor's pass, he had left one for you. It had *your* name on it; it wasn't for just anybody. Plus he'd paid the fine you owed for losing the first one. He's going ahead of us."

Dylan nodded slowly. He took another bite, and chewed thoughtfully. "But these rolls were put here in the last few minutes. If he had been here and put them in the closet *before* we got here, they wouldn't still be warm—we were up in that bell tower a long time."

"That's true," Clare agreed. "Well, then, sometimes he goes ahead of us, sometimes he follows us."

"But why?" Dylan asked. "He must know all about us. He must know we want to be authorized so we can come and go in Holiday whenever we like. Why doesn't he just stop and let us catch up to him? Or why didn't he stay when he brought this bread?" A shadow passed over Dylan's face. "You don't think he's just playing with us, do you?" he asked, and as soon as he said it, he knew the answer to his own question. He shook his head firmly. "No, he's not like that. I don't know why, but I'm sure he isn't." Clare felt the same certainty. "I don't know what he's doing, and I don't know why he's doing it, but I feel sure that whatever he does, it's got to be right. Or he wouldn't do it."

"Right," Clare agreed. "Now how about if we go sit down and actually eat a meal, instead of just standing here gulping down bread? Look, here are some of the most perfect peaches I've ever seen." Clare held them up. "And chunks of two different kinds of cheese to go with the bread. And some hard-boiled eggs—he even remembered the salt. And," Clare held up this final crowning touch, "two chocolates for each of us, and do they ever look good!"

The cousins carried the food out to the front lawn and sat on the grass, in the last rays of the setting sun. Just before Dylan began to eat, he paused and spoke very earnestly. "I don't know what he's doing, and I don't know why he's doing it," he repeated. "But Clare, I think the most horrible thing in the whole world would be to get to the end of this four-day visit and never have met the Founder."

10

Winter Wasteland

*D*ylan woke, startled. Had morning already come? Had he slept through his chance to speak to the stars about the Founder? As his drowsy mind cleared, a gentle breeze touched Dylan's arm with the unmistakable feel of outside air in the deepest night. It even smelled late. Reassured, Dylan realized that he had only thought day was dawning because the sky shone so brightly. The light came, however, not from a soon-to-rise sun, or from a full moon, but from countless stars, all of them nearer than Dylan had ever known stars to be and all of them very bright. "Clare," he whispered, in the same tone you would use in a church service when you really must say something, but it would be irreverent to speak right out loud. "Wake up. The stars are out."

Clare woke immediately and sat up. Then both children rose to their feet and stared at the stars.

Millions of them twinkled and glittered, more than they had ever seen on even the clearest night. The smallest stars appeared as tiny specks in the distant sky, but many others were so near that they appeared the size of marbles, and others still were close enough to seem the size of Dylan's hand. As he stood looking up, Dylan noticed a kind of a buzzing noise. He didn't remember hearing it earlier. But now—a strong, steady, solemn hum rang out. Dylan took his eyes from the stars long enough to quickly glance around the mountaintop. He could see nothing that would make such a sound. It must have been coming from the stars themselves.

As before, with the bells, Dylan found himself wondering what was the proper way to begin a conversation with a star. "Oh, stars," he began. He felt the old-fashioned sounding "Oh" was necessary, like when a character in a book addresses someone great and noble. "Oh, stars, please speak to us. We need your help." He sounded little, lonely, and unimportant. Would the stars even speak to him? Why should they? He remembered the bell's words: "I don't know that they'd be willing to speak with you."

For a long moment, it seemed that Dylan's words had traveled out to space and gotten lost. No answer came back. There was no sound except the star noise. Finally, the star that must have been the closest, since it was the brightest and appeared the largest, began to shimmer and to twinkle more brightly. *It really must be answering*, Dylan thought with excitement, although he heard nothing. Then he realized that the sound of his words and sounds from the stars would need time to travel the distance between them. He waited a little longer and finally heard the voice of the twinkling star. The only way Dylan could describe the star's voice later was by saying, "It sounded like a whispered roar. And the star was a lady. I'm sure of it."

Although the star's voice sounded as though it came from far, far away, it spoke distinctly. "We have one purpose," the star said slowly and with great gravity. "One grand, glorious purpose. If we can meet your need as we fulfill our purpose, we will gladly give you aid. But know this—nothing will ever deter us from doing what we were designed to do. We have done it for centuries, for millennia, yet we never finish and we never tire. We have occupied these same places in the sky, night after night, day after day, always doing the same work. We know no change. Yet we never grow weary. We feel only delight in this most solemn, most joyful task we have received." The words stopped, and Dylan realized that the shimmering of the star had also stopped, a moment or two before.

"What is that task?" Dylan asked and waited as his words found their way up to the stars.

Seconds before the large, bright star began to shimmer in reply, another little star grew brighter and more twinkly. Soon, Dylan heard a tiny, tinkling voice say, "He's not very loud, is he? Do you think that's the loudest he can talk?" and, then, without waiting for an answer, "Well, but he is so very, very little."

The largest star's words drowned out the rest of the small star's comments. "We announce to everyone that the Founder . . ." The star paused and Dylan's heart beat faster. The star's voice grew even more solemn, and at the same time a tremor of joy ran through it. "That the Founder—is. We announce to every person on earth—for where is the place where stars are never seen?—to them all, we announce that the Founder *is* and that he is marvelous. He does remarkable things, amazing things. Look at us, the stars, and know that the Founder is altogether wonderful. Nothing, no one, is so excellent as he."

Dylan felt wrapped in a warm blanket of deep, calm, solemn joy. He was growing accustomed to this sensation—it seemed to follow whenever anyone spoke of the Founder. He felt no need to say anything else, but then Clare whispered, "Can I ask something?"

He nodded, and Clare called out, "Oh star, why do we see so many star decorations in our Holiday vacations?"

The same long pause ensued, while the large star, and the little one near it, both began to shimmer at almost the same moment. The smaller voice reached Dylan and Clare first. They heard it say, "Oh, look! There's another one! Look how teeny they are!"

The larger voice replied to Clare's question. "When the Founder first came to rescue the citizens of the ancient town from their oppressive rulers, he gave one of us stars a task—a grave task, a glad task, a most serious and important task. One of us announced his coming to certain men who had been watching for him. And then, when the men went in search of him, that one showed them where to look."

Excitement seized Dylan as an idea came into his head. He did not even wait for the star to finish speaking completely when he burst out, "Do you think one of you could do that for us? We do so want to find the Founder! Our time's half gone already and it doesn't seem like we're any closer to finding him than when we first came."

Dylan paced impatiently as he waited for his words to travel the distance. He stopped when both stars, big and small, but again, the smaller one first, began their pre-speaking shimmer. "Isn't that cute?" squealed the smaller voice. "He wants one of us to go with him."

"That was one task, one time, for one star," the larger star responded. "Our task now is simply to announce that the Founder is. He has other, surer ways of bringing people to himself and of making known just what he is like. Those things are not our task. We do *our* task, and ours only. It is enough for us, and it is enough to fill all our long years with richness."

Dylan felt a little cloud of disappointment blow in and settle on the excitement he had felt, dampening it. The sky itself seemed to share his feelings. As the cousins had talked with the stars, the night breeze had grown stronger by degrees, bringing in clouds. Only a few clouds at first, but now more and more blew across the stars, blocking first some, then many, from sight. Dylan could not see the smaller star shimmer in preparation of speaking, but he soon heard it say, "Aww. Poor little thing. Do you think he'll find the Founder?"

The deepening cloud cover muted much of the large star's answer, but Dylan knew the answer by heart. "——don't find——Founder, ——finds you;——Founder——Finder, too." Then the growing cloud cover broke just long enough for the large star to send down one final message. By the time the words reached Dylan, the star was no longer visible at all. Very few stars remained visible, peeping through the growing blanket of thick cloud. The words themselves, however, arrived as crystal clear as ever. "In the morning, go down the mountain and travel north. Head for the winter."

Going back down the mountain proved to be much easier than going up had been. At times, both Dylan and Clare found their legs a little shaky, since their muscles were still complaining about yesterday's hard climb. In a few places on the downward path, where the ground sloped steeply and the surface under their feet felt treacherous, Dylan and Clare sat down and inched their way along. For the most part, though, they had little trouble descending. When they reached the single tree that had shaded Mr. Smith's refreshment stand, no trace of him or of his stand remained.

"Too bad," Clare joked. "*Now* we're going down instead of up. Now he would have let us have some refreshments."

"You know he never meant to give us anything," Dylan replied. "He just wanted to keep us from going up the mountain." Then Dylan added, under his breath, "I don't see why it's so important to him to keep us from the real Holiday."

"That's okay," Clare answered, not hearing Dylan's last comment. "We don't need refreshments anyway. It's so much cooler today. Where were these clouds yesterday, when we were going up?" The clouds that had rolled in last night, ending the children's conversation with the stars, had remained and thickened into a blanket, blotting out the sun completely.

"Cooler *is* better," Dylan agreed, "but the stars said to go north when we get to the bottom. If these clouds don't clear out a little bit, I'm not sure I'm going to know which way north is. I can't see the sun."

As it turned out, however, Dylan did not need the sun to help him choose the direction to take—a good thing, since the overcast sky had done nothing but darken as the children descended. Any question of which way to go melted away as soon as they could read the sign at the foot of the mountain. It said, "ROAD NORTH TO WINTERLAND MANUFACTURING, INC. ¼ MILE." It pointed back down the road, the way they had come from the candlemaker's shop.

Obediently, Clare headed down the road in the direction the sign indicated. Dylan stopped, though. He eyed the sign suspiciously and said, "That wasn't here yesterday." Stepping off the path, first on this side, then the other, he searched the area with his eyes, as though he hoped to see the one who had put up the sign. He saw no one. Shaking his head, he followed Clare.

The cousins traveled the quarter mile in no time, and found themselves at another sign, posted where a second smaller path branched off the one that led to Holiday Village. This sign said, "NORTH." Then, underneath that, the children read, "WINTERLAND MANUFACTURING, INC." and under that, in smaller print, "TINSEL AND FRESH ICICLES FOR SALE."

Without discussion, Dylan and Clare turned toward the north and continued walking. Immediately, a sharp gust of wind hit them head on, bringing a hint of winter frost. "Oooh," Clare laughed, pretending to shiver, "just like that. We turn

the corner toward Winterland and get a winter blast of wind."
A second gust followed the first, and a third came up after
that. The separate blasts of chill wind came more and more
quickly and finally turned into one constant gale from the
north. Clare made no jokes now. She walked with her arms
folded tightly across her chest for warmth. "Brr," she said. "I
wish I had my jacket."

Dylan thrust his hands as deeply into his jeans pockets as
he could, trying to keep them warm. The wind brought tears
to his eyes, and his nose had begun to run. He began walking
more quickly, and said to Clare, "Let's hurry. It will help us
stay warm. Plus we'll get there sooner."

Clare picked up the pace, but she wasn't sure about getting
"there" any sooner, because no "there" seemed anywhere
around. The land lay flat and open, producing nothing to

see in any direction. Perhaps someone farmed here in good weather—although Clare doubted that this particular piece of land ever had good weather. It felt as though nothing but winter ever touched this desolate spot. At any rate, nothing grew here now but an occasional clump of weeds. Wide open to the biting north wind, a barren wasteland stretched as far as the eye could see.

"Hey!" Dylan called out. "A snowflake!" One had just brushed against his nose—not that his nose would have felt it (it was too numb from the cold wind), but he had caught it out of the corner of his eye.

"So I see," Clare answered, delighted. "One just landed on my shirt." Clare always enjoyed snow. "Who ever would have thought it would start snowing? It's been so warm!"

"But I think we *should* have thought of it," Dylan answered. "The stars said that to head north was to head for the winter. And the sign said there'd be *fresh* icicles for sale. We may be in for it." Dylan had begun to understand that this trip to Holiday did not even faintly resemble any journey he had ever made before. Anything could happen here—and the things that *did* happen were not always comfortable. Indeed, as if in confirmation of his words, by the time Dylan had finished speaking, the snow was falling thick and fast. The few lifeless trees that stood here and there, isolated in the sterile fields, had begun to wear a coating of snow on their naked, outstretched branches.

"Let's go faster," Clare urged. She was beginning to crunch snow underfoot, and snow was getting into her shoes. Dylan, walking in front, had nothing to block the wind. It had already made his ears so cold that it felt as though they had frozen solid and could be broken off his head the way you can break icicles off the edge of a roof. Now the wind blew the falling snow into his face in stinging blasts of cold wetness. It also blew his thin shirt, useless against the wintry wind and growing wetter every minute, up against his skin.

Miserable as all this felt, Dylan had no time to notice it. Instead, he concentrated intently, trying to stay on the path, which was rapidly disappearing under the deepening snow. Faintly, Clare's voice came from behind. Although she walked right behind him, trying to step where he had already stepped to keep her feet out of the snow, when she called out to him, the wind blew her voice right back into her mouth. "Dylan," she called, "maybe we could go back to the candlemaker and borrow some warm clothes."

Dylan stopped and turned to face her, or she never would have heard him over the wind. "We can't," he answered. "I've lost the road. It's completely buried."

"What are we going to do?" Clare cried, and her voice carried a touch of desperation. "I'm freezing!"

"I don't know," Dylan answered, "but I think we'd better keep moving." He turned back around and walked on into the wind, trying to move in the general direction of where the path had been. The wind, blowing hard all this time already, whipped itself into a yet more bitter rage. It howled in its fury. The snow, not to be outdone, fell thicker, faster, coming down in almost solid sheets. The children could hardly see a few steps in front of them. Snowflakes, hurled by the angry wind, caught in their eyelashes and did not melt. With each step, their feet sank into new piles of snow.

Where Dylan and Clare lived, it snowed occasionally, but not often. They had never seen a blizzard. Clare thought she remembered reading that, where blizzards did occur, they could come up suddenly, catching people by surprise. *Is this a blizzard?* Clare wondered. Who ever would have thought that, in so short a time, the weather could change so drastically? Thinking about blizzards, Clare remembered that she had also read about people who had been caught out in blizzards and had actually frozen to death before they could reach shelter. Clare ran the two steps necessary to catch up to Dylan and grabbed his arm to get his attention. He turned and the sight of his red face with ice caught in his eyebrows and eyelashes did nothing to calm Clare's growing fear.

"D-D-Dylan." Between the cold and the fear, she could not help the stammering. "I'm scared. We c-c-can't stay out in this. It's too cold; it's too big."

He almost shouted at her, out of his frustration at having no solution, and his teeth chattered too. "I don't know what to d-d-do! I don't know where to go! I just know we'd better not stand still."

"But where are we going?" Clare wailed, her voice almost one with the wailing wind. "I'm soaked. I can't feel my toes!"

Dylan cast about in his mind for an idea of any kind, but the effort was fruitless. The minute of standing there, saying nothing, did, however, enable the cousins to hear a sound coming in faint bursts over the roar of the wind. "That can't be a motorcycle," Dylan muttered. "You can't ride a motorcycle through snow this deep."

"A snowmobile!" Clare cried. "I'll bet it's a snowmobile!" And she began to dance in her excitement. "What can we do? How can we make him see us?"

"I have a feeling it won't be that hard," Dylan answered, more to himself than to Clare. "And I bet I know who's on the snowmobile."

The engine noise grew louder. Soon, in the distance, against the dull gray and white of the storm, a bright splash of canary yellow appeared. Clare began waving her stiff arms to signal the driver. "Clare," Dylan cautioned, "you know who that's likely to be."

"*Don't* say that!" Clare moaned in her dismay at realizing what Dylan meant. "It *can't* be him! It just can't be!" But she stopped her waving and let her arm fall lifelessly.

It was, of course. The yellow snowmobile buzzed cheerfully to where Dylan and Clare stood, freezing, and came to a halt, the engine continuing to run. The rider wore a quilted snowsuit, thickly padded, and heavy waterproof mittens. The ends of his pants were stuffed into high snow boots. His face peeked out from under a furry hood. Mr. Smith lifted his goggles, then uncovered the part of his face hidden by a big scarf. He smiled as though he had just come upon others out for a little recreation, like himself. "Isn't this perfect weather for this kind of thing?" he beamed. "And what a gorgeous landscape, huh?" he chuckled. "If you like lots of nothing. Why, I'll bet the only thing you could grow on this piece of land is—*cold*!" He laughed at his own joke.

Mr. Smith pretended to look more closely at Dylan and Clare. "And I believe you've produced a bumper crop of that very thing!" He shook his head. "When are you children going to learn? You can't go off on these wild goose chases for towns that are just pretend. It keeps landing you into trouble. Look at you—you're soaked, you're shaking all over, there's ice on your faces—and there's no help in sight—nor *any* towns, make-believe or otherwise. Admit it—weren't you better off back at the Visitors' Center, just enjoying Holiday vacations once a year? This certainly isn't what you wanted, is it? Admit it—you never should have come. Then I'll happily load you onto my snowmobile—" Mr. Smith inched to the very front of the snowmobile's long seat, making room for additional riders, "and I'll have you someplace warm in a jiffy." He tapped the seat. "This even opens, and I have blankets inside you could wrap up in for the ride back."

Straightening up as best he could, Dylan tensed his muscles to try to make them stop shivering. He clenched his teeth together to silence their chattering. Before he could voice his firm "No," however, the little man leaned toward him, and said, softly, "But what about Clare?"

Dylan glanced around at Clare. Her body shook uncontrollably. Her clothing and every hair on her head dripped icy water. He wondered if her mind was being affected, because he saw her looking all around, absently.

"It's all well and good to try to play the stubborn hero yourself and prove to us all how tough you can be," Mr. Smith purred, "but what about your little cousin? You don't have much time, you know," and his voice grew insistent. "She needs to get out of those clothes. If she doesn't, she's going to end up as frozen and dead as everything else in this place."

Dylan's own mind seemed to be moving very slowly. Was Mr. Smith really speaking in slow motion? Because that was how it sounded. What was the argument? Oh, yes, Clare. Clare needed to get away from here for some reason. What was the reason? He turned to Clare to ask her—but she was no longer standing there. She had moved away from him and from the man and was plowing awkwardly through the snow. Dylan felt a touch of irritation. *She can't go anywhere now,* he thought, *we're supposed to go somewhere with Mr. Smith.*

"Oh, dear, Dylan," Dylan heard the man call, and there was an unusual note of panic in the voice. "I'm afraid it's already too late for Clare. You won't be able to save her now. Save yourself before it's too late. Come with me; get on the snowmobile. Clare would want you to. Come on, Dylan."

Mr. Smith's suggestion jolted Dylan's fading thoughts into a fresh state of alert. Leave Clare here and go with that man? Unthinkable! But where in the world was she going? *There's nothing else to do,* Dylan thought. *I've got to go with her.* And without another word to the man on the snowmobile, he turned stiffly and followed after Clare.

11

Winterland Manufacturing

O ver the howling of the wind, Dylan heard Mr. Smith calling, urgently. "Don't be a fool, Dylan, come back! Clare doesn't know what she's doing. She'll just lead you off to die in this wasteland!" Then Dylan saw it. Clare was heading toward a little shack, built of gray wood, almost invisible in the winter storm. It had no door, just three walls leaning crazily and a roof sagging under its burden of snow. Small as it was, the shack's interior remained dark, invisible. As soon as Dylan caught sight of the shack, he heard the angry revving of the snowmobile's motor as the man sped away. *He knew this was here*, Dylan thought dully. *He didn't want me to see it. That's why he tried to keep me from following Clare.*

Clare had disappeared through the doorway. Dylan followed. Inside, the floor sloped steeply down, under the far wall, and it led down a well-lit tunnel, farther in than Dylan could see. A small sign pointed down the hall to "Winterland Manufacturing, Inc." Dylan and Clare stumbled down this sharply descending hallway. At least no snow fell in the tunnel, nor did they have to wade through any on the floor. They were already so wet and miserable, though, that they scarcely noticed. Their hearts sank when they finally reached the end of the corridor and found that it opened onto a snow-covered clearing, with more snow falling from overhead.

There was a difference though. Here the snow fell gently in great flakes. No wind blew. And the clearing floor had been swept clean, so that only a thin layer of snow lay on the ground, not deep piles. The clearing had been made in the center of a deep wood. Armies of large dark trees marched right up to the edges and stood all around. Dylan and Clare saw movement and bustle at the center of the clearing, near a number of buildings. From this center, a creature hurried now to meet them. As it approached, the children recognized it as a penguin, waddling as quickly as its short legs would allow. As it drew near, it called back over its shoulder, "Visitors! Bring something warm! And *hurry!*"

Two other figures, shorter but much faster, separated themselves from the bustle at the center of the

clearing and bounded after the penguin, and a third figure, taller than any of the others and pulling something behind it, followed too. Just as the penguin reached Dylan and Clare, the two Saint Bernards (for that was what they turned out to be) reached them as well. On their backs, they carried bundles, each tied with a big obvious bow. Little barrels were attached to the collars around their necks. The penguin pointed to one of the bows with his wing. "Go ahead," he urged. "Pull the string." Dylan pulled one with his stiff red fingers, and Clare pulled the other. The bundles easily came off the dogs, into the children's hands, opening into thick, woolen blankets. Gratefully, Dylan and Clare wrapped blankets around their shivering bodies. "And those are thermoses on the dog collars. There's hot chocolate in them. Just pull the collar apart; it's Velcro," the penguin added. The children obeyed, and soon chocolaty steam rose into their faces and their frozen hands wrapped around warm mugs.

The penguin made a courtly bow. "Welcome to Winterland Manufacturing. We excel in tinsel and fresh icicles. We're delighted to have your company." Then, a little less formally, he added, "Looks like you had a hard time finding the place, eh?"

Dylan tried to answer, but his tongue felt like a thick wooden block in his mouth and he could hardly feel his jaw, it was so cold. The penguin held up a wing to stop him. "Ah-ah-ah," he said. "Time to chat later. Right now, it's hot baths, hot soup, and naps in a warm bed for you." By then, the last figure to come toward them, a reindeer, had arrived. It pulled a sled, more blankets piled on the seat. Again with his wing, the penguin indicated the sled. "In you go," he said. "He'll have you somewhere toasty in a jiffy." The children clambered into the sled and under the blankets on the seat. With another bow, the penguin waved the reindeer on.

Several hours later, having been thawed in warm baths, strengthened by hot soup, and refreshed by long naps under thick quilts, Dylan and Clare felt like new people. Upon rising from their naps, they had found heavy parkas, fur-lined boots, mittens, and woolen caps in just their sizes. Now, wearing these, they followed the penguin around the center of the clearing on a tour of Winterland Manufacturing, Inc. "Just one question," Dylan was saying, "how did you happen to have all these warm things here, in just our sizes?"

"Oh, well, we do get visitors, you know," the penguin replied. "And the Founder likes to make sure that, when they come, they have exactly what they need. Have you heard of the Founder?"

"Oh, yes, that's why we're here," Dylan replied. "Originally, we just came to try to see the real Holiday, and to get authorized to come whenever we want to. So it was actually the Founder we were trying to find, since he is the only who could authorize us."

Here the penguin interrupted. "Oh, you can't find the Founder," he said quickly, before Dylan could stop him, "he finds you."

"Right," Dylan said. "That's what we've heard. Everywhere we've gone, we've heard more about the Founder, and he even seems to be kind of following us—or going ahead of us—or something. Anyway, I get the feeling that he knows all about us—"

The penguin glanced sharply at Dylan. "Of course he does," he interposed.

"—and the more I learn about him, the more I'd really like to meet *him*, even more than I want to get authorized to go to the real Holiday. I don't suppose he's here somewhere? The stars said they couldn't show us where he was, but they said we should come here." And Dylan looked around, half-hoping, half-certain of disappointment.

"Well," the penguin replied, "I can at least show you all around. Like everything else in Holiday, Winterland Manufacturing is here in his honor. If you don't actually meet him here, you'll at least learn more about him." Dylan and Clare agreed, and the penguin puffed himself up proudly.

"Whether it's at the Visitor's Center at vacation time or in the town of Holiday itself, you'll find tinsel garlands and icicle decorations. Well," and the penguin's chest puffed even fuller, "this is where all those decorations come from. Right here. We make them." He waddled into a long barn, followed by the cousins. "This is where the caribou sleep at night. Right now they're all out at work, although they'll be coming home soon. It's getting on toward evening. They go out each day, into the forest, and select the very finest icicles they can find. Long, silvery, beautiful—that's the criteria. Only the best icicles can bear the Winterland Manufacturing name. The caribou reach up into the tree branches and carefully remove the very best icicles." The three exited the barn, opposite the door they had entered, walked a few steps, and entered a smaller building.

"This is the kennel for the Saint Bernards," the penguin explained. "They go out with the caribou, carrying insulated padded containers strapped to their backs. The caribou lay the icicles very carefully into those containers, to be brought

back here." The penguin led Dylan and Clare out of the kennel and to another building, far larger than any of the others.
As the door of this building opened, a wave of noise poured
out, greeting the newcomers.

Upon stepping inside, Dylan and Clare understood the
reason for all the noise. Just inside the door, a huge company
of penguins scurried about, all obviously very busy, and chattered contentedly to one another as they worked. At the far
end of the long building, large polar bears shuffled about,
also clearly busy with something. Near the large exit doors,
walruses slid over the floor, kept wet for their sake, with some
task of their own. Although Clare would not have thought
it possible, the penguin's chest swelled even larger here. "In
this factory, we have our unique, prize-winning, secret process—which, sorry, I'm afraid I can't show you—for turning
regular frozen, meltable icicles into permanent, non-melting
icicles—still long, silvery, and beautiful, of course, but in no
danger of disappearing into a little puddle on the floor—the

very icicles you will find as decorations in Holiday. That's what the penguins do."

The penguin led them on to the bears' area. Each polar bear had a pile of icicles next to him. One by one, he took the icicles from the pile and strung them together into a long garland. Two polar bears held up one of these tinsel garlands, just completed, making sure that all the icicles stayed securely fastened. "Tinsel garlands, that's the polar bears' job," the penguin stated, leading them past and over to the walruses. "Walruses are in charge of packaging," he explained. Walruses on one side of the aisle were busy putting icicles into blue boxes, while walruses on the other side put garlands in silver boxes.

The penguin led the children back out of the building. Right outside the door, a number of small sleds waited in rows. "Tomorrow, husky dogs will use these sleds to take a shipment of garlands and icicles into Holiday. Too late for any more to go out today, though." The penguin glanced at the setting sun. "In fact, it's quitting time. Excuse me for a second." He stepped back into the large noisy building and made a loud whistle.

(*Is that just a loud penguin noise?* Clare wondered. *Or does he actually have a whistle?* She never did find out.) The penguin rejoined them. "Let's go get a bite to eat. Of course, you'll stay the night?" he asked.

"Thank you, yes, I guess we'd better," Dylan replied. "I'm a little worried about going back through that frozen wasteland, even in daylight. I certainly don't want to at night. But then, tomorrow's our last day. Our passes will be used up at the end of the day. And I'm not sure we'll ever find the Founder—or get found by him," he added hastily, before the penguin could interject the familiar jingle.

"Not to worry about the frozen wasteland," the penguin said, as they walked into a low log cabin that served as a dining hall and sat down. "You'll go out with the dog sleds, riding one of them in fact. And you can keep all the warm clothes until you don't need them anymore. Just put them all back on the dog sled when you take them off. And not to worry about the Founder, either. I'm sure you're on the right track. Or he's on the right track." And the penguin chuckled and winked, but would say no more about it.

The children ordered chili and the penguin ordered fish. As they waited for their meal, Clare asked the penguin, "Do you have any idea why someone would work really hard at trying to keep people from ever finding the Founder and getting authorized?" And she explained about Mr. Smith and his snowmobile, along with all the other encounters with him they had had.

"Well," the penguin answered thoughtfully, "the Founder didn't just rescue the town to let it run along on its own, you know. He *rules* the town. He is its King. And he requires those who live in the town to obey the great Emperor as well. My guess is that your Mr. Smith is like the Darkness Dwellers. They don't want to leave the darkness, because there, they're free to do what *they* want to do, with no one telling them they shouldn't do it. Mr. Smith probably thinks like this: If there's no *real* Holiday, there's no real Founder. If there's no real Founder, there's no King. And if there's no King, I don't have to obey anyone other than myself. So when people try to find the real Holiday and the real Founder, he wants to stop them."

Clare agreed that the penguin's theory made sense. Then their food came, and no one said anything for a few minutes while they all ate hungrily. Spending so much time outside on a cold day had given Dylan and Clare quite an appetite. Once they had slowed down a bit, Dylan said politely, "Thank you for the tour. It was very interesting. The icicles really are beautiful, and it's amazing, that secret process you have for making them non-melting. But, I'm not sure I see what they have to do with the Founder or why we always see them on our Holiday vacations."

"Well," the penguin explained, "legend has it that the Founder first came to the town that is now Holiday in the dead of winter. The funny thing is, as much good historical evidence as we have about so much else that has to do with the Founder, no one really knows what day he first showed up. It probably wasn't winter at all. But the dead of winter would have been a really appropriate time for him to come, wouldn't it, because the conditions of the people he came to were certainly winter-like. Think about it. In winter, everything's dark, dreary, and dead. Days are short, and people feel depressed. There's very little sun, so nothing grows. Plants go dormant, producing nothing. Tree branches are naked and they can't bear any fruit. Winter's a wasteland, like the one you came through. Before the Founder rescued them, those he rescued lived in a winter of their own making. They were hopeless; they were lifeless. They could produce nothing worth anything at all. Even if they'd wanted to return to the good Emperor they'd rebelled against, they would have been able to bring him absolutely nothing as a gift to win his favor. The Founder came and changed all that. He burst in upon them all like springtime. He brought light and life and worked so many changes in them and in their town that they became wonderfully productive. Now, the real citizens of Holiday grow all kinds of fruit and produce all kinds of gifts for the Emperor, gifts that he not only accepts, but accepts with delight. So people decorate Holiday homes and Holiday vacation spots with icicles and garlands, reminders of the winter barrenness from which the Founder rescued them."

"What about the Founder?" Dylan asked. "Does anyone give *him* gifts? He's the one who has done all this for these people."

"Oh, gifts for the Emperor, gifts for the Founder—it's all really the same you know," the penguin answered vaguely.

Dylan *didn't* know. But he was only half listening. "I think *I'd* like to give the Founder a gift," he said. He looked the penguin full in the face. "What would you give to the Founder?" he asked. "And how would I get it to him?"

"Well," the penguin began. "I can't tell you how to find him to give it to him, because, well, you know," and the penguin glanced at Dylan who nodded. "But I think you could leave it for him at the Holiday chapel. Many people who find him—or, who are found by him—" and even the penguin seemed confused for a minute—"anyway, it often happens there. At the chapel. And I really can't tell you *what* to give him. But you said that on this whole trip, he's been going ahead of you, or behind you, or whatever, and seems to know all about you. He's probably been providing for you all along the way, hasn't he?" And the penguin nodded at Dylan's fur-lined boots. "I rather suspect that you'll find giving him a gift to be the same." The penguin, who seemed to feel important when he talked in riddles and who seemed to like feeling important, would say no more. Dylan and Clare finished their chili thoughtfully, told the penguin good night, and went off to bed.

The children rose early to catch the departing dog sleds out of Winterland. They had already climbed onto a pile of boxes on one of the sleds when the penguin waddled out to see them off. "The dogs can only go as far as there's snow, of course," he told them. "There's a tiny train station just before the edge of Winterland. That's where the sleds stop. The icicle shipment finishes its journey by freight train. That's where you'll get off and give back the warm clothes. From there, just follow the road—it won't be far into Holiday."

"Would that be the *real* Holiday?" Dylan asked. The penguin nodded. "Not the Visitors' Center and not Holiday Village?" The penguin shook his head. "The real Holiday?" The penguin nodded again. "Well, that's good!" Dylan said. "And not a day too soon. Our passes expire today at sunset."

Just then, the sled the children sat on started off with a jerk, and Dylan and Clare grabbed at each other to keep from tumbling off into the snow. "And then once you're there," the penguin called, "head for the chapel." He waved his wing, growing smaller and smaller as the caravan of sleds moved steadily away at a trot.

The brisk pace in the early morning breeze caused Clare to reach up to pull her hood more tightly closed against her neck. Dylan adjusted his wool cap over his ears. He looked thoughtful. Clare wondered if he was worrying about their passes expiring before they could get authorized. "So," she said, "we're finally going to be in Holiday! Aren't you excited?"

"Hm?" Dylan said absently. Then he realized what she had said, and his face brightened. "Oh. Right. That will be good." The thoughtful look reappeared almost immediately. "But I don't care nearly as much about Holiday as I did a few days ago. It's the Founder I want to see. And I really want to get him a gift. What do you think I could get him?"

Clare was thinking about how to answer when the lead dog on the lead sled gave a short sharp bark and began to run. The other dogs all began to run as well. The cold wind blew into Clare's face, stinging her eyes and numbing her lips. The wind roared in her ears, even in spite of the warm hood. Talking became impossible, and the two cousins huddled together on top of the sled for the rest of the ride.

After some time, Dylan caught sight of a line in the distance that ran across the snow. At almost the same time, the dogs slackened their pace. As they approached the line in the snow, they slowed to a walk and finally stopped at what looked something like a child's playhouse. It was a tiny building, with a roof no higher than Dylan's shoulder. "Oh my goodness," Clare laughed. "When the penguin said a 'tiny train station,' he meant it! Look, Dylan, it's a *model* train." Indeed, it was— a *large* model train, but a model train nonetheless.

The snow was much less deep here. The wind had died and the sun shone brightly. Once the sled had stopped, the children realized that their coats and gloves had become much too warm. Even so, after the cold, bracing ride, they found their arms and legs stiff and hard to move as they crawled back down from the pile of boxes on the sled. Once they were on the ground, they had gloves, hats, coats, scarves to remove, fold up, and place on the sled. It must have been because they were busy with those things that they failed to notice where the team of short men in red uniforms came from. They could not have all fit inside that tiny building! The little men nodded at Dylan and Clare, then got to work unloading small packages from the dog sleds and filling the model train's freight cars. Dylan and Clare thanked the dogs harnessed to the sled they had ridden, then started off down the road. It led up a little hill, and, as soon as they'd topped the hill and started down the other side, the snow was gone. The sun shone, the birds sang, the grass grew—and Winterland was but a memory.

Suddenly, Dylan gave a little cry of dismay. "Clare!" he said. "I don't have any money. I'd forgotten about my wallet getting stolen."

"So?" Clare answered. "We should be okay—we only have one day left, and so far, we really haven't had to buy *anything*; whatever we've needed has just been there for us, all along the way."

"I mean for a gift," Dylan said. "How can I give the Founder something when I don't have any money?"

"I have a little bit," Clare answered, "and you can have it if you want, but—doesn't it seem like the Founder's not really the kind of person you could *buy* a gift for?"

"What do you mean?" Dylan asked.

"Well, think about it, what would you buy him?" Clare persisted.

Dylan thought for a moment, started to say something twice, but stopped himself both times. Finally, he answered, "I see what you mean. What would he want? I'm sure there's nothing he needs. *He's* been giving *us* everything we've needed. But that's just it! That's why I *have* to give him something. In fact, Clare," and Dylan's face grew animated with this new idea, "maybe that's why he takes so long to be found. Maybe he only wants to authorize people who really appreciate what he does. Maybe he watches to see which people show appreciation and those are the ones he authorizes." And Dylan muttered, more under his breath than to Clare, "I've got to give him something." He turned back to Clare. "Maybe we can find something in one of the Holiday Village shops. How much do you have? I'll pay you back when we get home."

Clare took her wallet out of her pocket and handed it to Dylan. "Not much, but you can have all that's in there. But I still say, even if I had loads of money in there, it wouldn't be enough to buy something for the Founder. I just don't think he's like that."

Dylan and Clare soon arrived back at Holiday Village. Clare followed Dylan as he wandered into, then back out of, every shop on the street. Sometimes his face would light up for a moment or he'd pick something up to examine it more closely, but each time, he'd shake his head, thinking how this just could not be good enough to give to the Founder.

Finally, Dylan exited the last shop, Clare at his heels. Dylan took a few steps away from the street to a weathered little bench sitting off by itself. He sank onto this bench, discouraged. "I can't give him anything," he moaned. "So I guess I'll never find him. He won't want to see me when I have nothing to give. He'll think I don't appreciate all he's done and he won't authorize me."

"Dylan," Clare was actually scolding her cousin now, something she did not often do. "You're making all that up. No one has said the Founder's like that. No one's said you have to give him something before he'll see you. You've just come up with that yourself and talked yourself into it!"

"Clare," Dylan answered, speaking as though he were talking to a very young child who did not understand much, "you never get something for nothing. Everything always costs. It may be that you can't really *pay* for what the Founder does for you, but you have to contribute *something*. That's just the way things work."

12

A Gift for the Founder

When Dylan, already frustrated, heard Clare laugh, he snapped. "What's so funny?"

"You are, dear," said a quavery little voice, from behind the bench he sat on and near the ground. At that moment, Dylan realized it had not been Clare who had laughed. The laugh had not even sounded like Clare's. "You sound *so* sure of yourself," the sweet voice continued, "but you're *so* wrong."

Both Dylan and Clare spun around on the bench, so that their backs were to the road, and looked down at the ground. A small plant with dark green leaves and one large bright red flower grew there. "A poinsettia!" Clare cried.

"That's right," replied the plant, in a voice that sounded like that of Dylan and Clare's grandmother. "My name's Penny. And you, dear," she said, turning to Clare, "understand much better how the Founder thinks than your friend there."

"He's my cousin," Clare answered, and then, generously, considering how short Dylan had been with her, "and he's my friend too. His name's Dylan, and I'm Clare."

"Well, let me tell you something, Dylan," Penny said, "something about gifts for the Founder. Do you ever remember seeing poinsettias like me on your Holiday vacations?"

Dylan, still cross from his long fruitless search, only nodded. Clare hurried to give a more civil reply. "Sure," she said, "they're everywhere. They line some of the streets, they're in houses and stores, sometimes they're even in the church."

The poinsettia plant moved up and down slightly. *That must be the way a plant nods its head since it doesn't have a head to nod*, Dylan thought, becoming interested in spite of himself.

"There's a story about poinsettias and about how they came to be used in Holiday," Penny went on. "The story has it that a particular village had planned a big celebration for the Founder. It would be held at the village church, and every single villager would bring the Founder a gift. For months, all the villagers had been planning

and preparing. Farmers had grown prize vegetables to bring. Shepherds had chosen their most perfect sheep. Women had sewn, knitted, or embroidered scarves and sashes of the most beautiful colors imaginable. Rich people had saved all year, then gone on journeys to purchase wonderful jewels to give. Everyone had something and no one planned to give less than his or her very best. But, there was one very, very poor woman who had nothing to give. She had no money with which to buy anything. She had no food to prepare as a gift—why, she herself had not eaten a real meal all day. She lived alone in a tiny rented room with no yard in which to grow anything. She had absolutely nothing for a gift.

"The day of the Founder's celebration had come, and all the villagers were streaming up the hill to the church with their gifts, singing and laughing. The woman could not stay away, even though she had no gift. She loved the Founder and was as grateful as anyone for all he had done. It broke her heart to have nothing to give him on this special day for him. So she followed along on the edges of the crowd, but, as the others hurried faster when they drew near the village church, the poor woman's feet moved more and more slowly. How could she go in the door with no gift in her hands? How could she just stand there when everyone else was moving up to the front of the church to set down a gift? At last, left alone on the dusty road when everyone else had passed, she sank down by the side of the road and began to cry. Legend has it that her tears fell on a weed growing by the road, and they washed the dust from its bright red flowers. The woman stopped her crying to look at the flower, and realized how beautiful it was. Gladly, she gathered it up and hurried on to the church. The flower would be her gift. She was sure it would bring the Founder joy; in fact, she rather believed the Founder himself had left it there for her to give him as a gift."

Penny paused. "She was right, of course; he *had* left it there for her to give. And if you're thinking that that flower must have been a poinsettia, *you're* right, too. When you see poinsettias all around Holiday, you should let them remind you that the only way anyone can ever give to the Founder is by giving back to him what he's given first.

"You can't give him anything he needs," the perky plant continued. "He doesn't need anything. You can't give him anything he doesn't have; he has everything. You can't earn his gifts and you can't pay him back for them. Think back to when you were little and you wanted to give a gift to your mom. Of course, she loved it that you wanted to give her a gift. But the only way you could do it was to go to your mom, ask her for some money, then use *her* money to go buy her a gift. When you gave it to her, she was delighted, wasn't she? But, when you think about it, it was almost like a gift *from* your mom *to* your mom! That's how it will be with the Founder. He'll show you gifts he wants from you. But you won't have what it takes to give them. He'll give *you* all you need to give *him* a gift. So stop wasting your last day here *shopping* and go on to the chapel."

Dylan, ashamed of his previous rude behavior, spoke up. "I'm sorry I was rude earlier—to you, too," he added, turning to Clare. "Thank you very much for telling us all that. I'll do like you say, and I'll just wait to see what the Founder wants, *and* how he gives it to me to give back to him. Your story was very helpful, and I'm glad we ran into you."

The poinsettia giggled, sounding like a sweet little old lady. "Of course, you *didn't* 'run into me,'" she corrected. "The

Founder put me here to wait for you." And the whole plant moved gently from side to side—(*which must be*, thought Dylan, *the way a plant shakes its head when it has no head to shake*). "Are you *ever* going to get this, young man?" she added so quietly that Dylan was not even sure she had said it.

Since Dylan and Clare had searched every store in Holiday Village, their conversation with Penny had taken place at the very end of the little village that lay just outside of the real city of Holiday. Now they had only to cross the short stretch of open road between Holiday Village and the real town to finally be in the beautiful city they had looked down on from the roadside overlook. They hurried along this stretch of road, eager to finally reach their destination. They kept up such a brisk pace that, when they spoke, their sentences came out in jerky little bursts.

"You know," Dylan said, "annoying as it was—back at the beginning—to have to go—the long way to—Holiday,—I'm glad it worked out—that way. I'm sure—we'll appreciate—Holiday—much more now—that we've gone through so much—to get to it."

"And," Clare added, also panting because of their speed, "look how much we've learned—about the Founder. We wouldn't have known—any of that—if we'd come the easy way."

"Yes," Dylan agreed in a soft, serious voice, more to himself than to Clare, "and the Founder really seems to be the main point. I'll bet you can't know the real Holiday if you don't understand about the Founder."

A few more moments of quick walking and Dylan and Clare passed the sign that read "Holiday City Limits." Several more steps and they stepped through the city gate that stood open, inviting. There they stopped, overwhelmed with the wonder of what lay before them. Buildings of all kinds greeted their eyes. Grand elegant halls, simple cozy cottages, tall imposing towers, exquisitely styled mansions, inviting little shops and cafes—all were different, but every one was beautiful. Each building had its own yard, landscaped to be an extension of the building. The great, imposing structures sat in expansive green lawns, bordered by well-trimmed hedges. Each smaller house or shop, even the most simple, had its own garden, however tiny, full of flowers of all kinds. The streets, obviously cared for with loving attention, were lined with every sort of tree. Pine and fir trees, flowering fruit trees, full shade trees, all grew along the streets.

Each tree with blossoms, each evergreen tree, each flower growing in a yard, gave off its own strong, pure, glad fragrance. Rather than overwhelming Dylan and Clare with one great jumbled smell, each fragrance seemed to stand out on its own so that first the cousins smelled pine, then rose, then orange blossom, then lavender. Nor were plants the only sources of scent. Every delicious food that ever produced a smell to make one's mouth water wafted on the Holiday air: melting choco-late, baking bread, spicy cider, toasted nuts, and roasting meats of all kinds. Over it all came the scent of the outdoors on a clear, crisp morning with, just lightly, a trace of the smell of smoke rising from a fireplace.

"Mmm," Clare breathed. "I think I could eat some lunch right about now."

"Sh," Dylan said, "listen." Listen they did, and each sound, like each fragrance, stood out sharply on its own, first one and then another, never degenerating into one big background noise. First voices singing in exquisite harmony, then precisely tuned strings; next, the deep solemn tone of large bells and the cheery tinkling of little chimes; then the clear call of a horn followed by delighted laughter—from everywhere and from nowhere in particular the sounds poured forth.

Clare shook her head, amazed. Then she asked her cousin, "What do you want to do first, Dylan?"

The question broke in on Dylan's concentrated wonder. Im-mediately, he began to search for signs giving directions. "Go to the chapel, of course," he answered. "I want to see if the Founder will come. The penguin said that's the place where people most often meet up with him. Of course, I still don't have a gift. . . ." The last words were under Dylan's breath and trailed off, the sentence left unfinished, as Dylan saw a signpost. One arm of the sign pointed to Holiday Chapel, and Dylan hurried off in that direction. Clare, still hungry, but thinking to herself that, after all, this was really Dylan's trip, followed.

For the first time on this whole trip, the children found a place easily. The chapel building itself proved to be one of the plainest in the city. It resembled, almost identically, the church in the Visitors' Center part of Holiday. The chapel sat empty for the moment, since no services were being held. Nonetheless, as soon as Dylan stepped into the building, he felt a deep sense of expectation. It seemed like a time to be his most serious, yet, at the same time, joy fuller than any he had ever felt before bubbled up inside him. "Clare," he whispered, wondering why he was whispering and yet realizing, as soon as he had wondered it, that whispering was just *right* somehow. "I'm *sure* the Founder will come. I'm sure we'll find him. I just know it."

Dylan sat down on a bench in the back of the room. Clare marveled at this new side of Dylan. He wasn't the type to sit and wait. He liked to be out *doing*, making things happen. Yet Clare could see that Dylan was prepared to sit right there and wait his entire final day of admission to Holiday, if necessary, to see the Founder. She had the good sense to realize that, though this was not like Dylan and though she herself was hungry, this was the right thing. This was what Dylan needed to do. So Clare sat down to wait beside him.

13

Found!

ylan had been sitting in the stillness long enough to have lost all sense of time, when, suddenly, he heard footsteps outside and the clicking sounds of the doorknob turning. His breath caught in his throat and a rush of emotion swept up inside. Joy, hope, shyness, fear, gladness, anxiety—all surged through him at once in a powerful wave that left him feeling light-headed. He grabbed at Clare's arm. "Here he comes," he whispered, and, together, they turned to watch the Founder walk in the door.

Slowly, the doorknob turned. Slowly, someone pushed open the door. Slowly, a man's head peeked around the door, followed by his body. The man was more than a little rumpled. He appeared to have forgotten to comb his hair that morning. One long sleeve of his shirt was rolled up a turn or two while the other sleeve was pushed clear up to his elbow. A pencil had been thrust behind each ear. He held a roll of paper that slipped a little in his hand as he stepped through the door, causing it to unroll almost all the way to the floor. He began to roll it back up while at the same time peering around the room over the tops of half-glasses. His face lit up when his eyes fell on Dylan and Clare.

Dylan felt confused. "Are—are you—you're not the Founder, are you?" he asked.

The man threw back his head and laughed. "Oh dear me, no," he replied. "Do I *look* like the Founder?"

"Well," Dylan replied, "you don't look like how I expect the Founder to look, but then, I don't really know *what* he looks like. I've never seen him."

The man became more serious. "Yes, well, neither have I," he said.

"But do you know the Founder?" Dylan asked, hopefully. "Did he send you?"

"Send me?" The man considered. "Well, yes, in a way I guess you could say that."

"But he didn't send you specifically to look for *us*, Dylan and Clare?" Dylan said, growing less hopeful by the minute that this man was here to help them meet the Founder.

"Dylan and Clare," the man muttered thoughtfully. Then, again, "Dylan and Clare. I don't *remember* those names—but then, I have so much to remember. It's a wonder I don't forget everything!" He unrolled the large roll of paper again, a little at a time, skimming over it with his eyes. "Nothing on here about anyone

named Dylan and Clare. No, I don't think I've been told any-thing about you," he concluded. "But," less thoughtfully and much more brightly, "I'm pleased to make your acquaintance. Name's Mert," and he stepped forward, thrusting out his hand to shake Dylan's and Clare's. They rose and shook his hand.

"I came in hoping to find some volunteers," Mert explained, "but I see there's no one here—except you, of course," he added, hastily. "I don't suppose you'd want to volunteer?" he asked with the only half-hopeful air of one who has often been turned down.

"To do what?" Clare asked. She knew they would have to tell him "no," but the disheveled little man seemed nice, and she hated to just say it outright.

"Make my deliveries," he answered, "do my chores. There's so much *stuff*—people are always very generous with their *stuff*. Problem is, when it's time to take it where it's needed and actually use it to help people, everyone's always too busy. Oh, I know how it is," he hastened to add, in the manner of one unwilling to complain, "schedules are so hectic these days. And they all really *are* generous. But it's just too much for one man to do. How will I ever do it all?" Reminded of his dilemma, Mert ran his fingers through his hair in a despairing gesture that left his hair even messier than before.

"What kind of stuff do you deliver?" Clare asked politely, still stalling to avoid having to say no.

"Why, step out here and see," Mert invited, opening wide the door and stepping back to make room for Dylan and Clare to pass. Dylan and Clare moved to the door and looked out. A small flatbed truck with a bright green cab sat, idling, at the curb. Wooden rails had been built around the truck bed so things could be carried without falling out. All sorts of things filled this truck bed: boxes, bags of groceries, pieces of furniture, several bicycles of different sizes, a lawn mower and yard tools, a vacuum cleaner, even a refrigerator.

"A lot of these things have been donated as gifts for people who, at least for the moment, are unable to provide them for themselves," Mert explained. "Those things I need to deliver. Some of the things—the lawn mower, for instance, are mine for helping with. Some folks don't need food or things, but their health is too poor to take care of chores around the house. So those people I need to do a little work for." Mert shook his head, and, again, ran his fingers through his hair. "But I don't know how I'll get it all done by the end of the day." He looked pleadingly at Dylan and Clare. "You don't want to help me out, do you?" he asked, with obvious apprehension that they would tell him no.

Clare glanced at Dylan. To her surprise, he was stepping out the door resolutely and replying, "Sure. We'll help," then, turning to Clare, "That's okay with you, Clare, isn't it?"

"Sure it's okay with me," said Clare. "I'd be happy to help. But, Dylan, what about the Founder? What about getting authorized? This is your last day."

"Hey, Mert," Dylan called. Mert, elated at having found some volunteers, had hurried to the driver's side of the cab and opened the door. With one foot already on the floor of the cab, he paused before springing up to the driver's seat, and looked over his shoulder at Dylan. "How long do you think we'll be," Dylan asked, "if all three of us work together?"

"Why, if we make really good time, we may be able to get it all done today!" Mert seemed quite cheerful about this prospect.

"Do you think there's any chance we could work really fast and be done *before* the end of the day?" Dylan asked.

Mert's foot came back out of the truck cab, and he turned to face Dylan. He glanced at the abundance in the back of the truck, looked over his long list, and shook his head. "I don't know," he said slowly, "there's an awful lot here. We can push for that, but I can't guarantee anything." Then he added reluctantly, "If you have another appointment, I suppose you'd better not chance it. You might be late."

"That's okay," Dylan brushed off Mert's suggestion with a wave of his hand. "It's okay if we're late."

Shocked, Clare whispered, "Dylan, what do you mean it's okay?"

"It just is," Dylan answered. "I'm sure it is. I'm sure that we should do this. I think it's what the Founder would want. I think it's what the Founder would *do* if he were here. But, let's hurry!" Dylan said this louder, so Mert would hear too. "It would be really good to be back within an hour or two before sunset."

"Then step to it, let's go!" cried Mert, jumping up into the driver's seat. Relief at not losing his new volunteers had obviously given him a fresh burst of energy. Dylan and Clare scrambled onto the bench seat of the cab. Mert put the truck into gear and they rattled off down the street.

The truck stopped first at a small house inhabited by a very old man and his wife. Mert explained that the couple had adopted their three young grandchildren when the children's parents had died. They had been faithfully providing them with food and shelter, but they had no extra money for playthings. So out of the truck came a large doll, several books, some cars and trucks, a ball, and a wagon.

Then the truck drove on to the home of a mother of four small children. She lay sick in bed. Dylan and Clare helped to unload a great pot of soup, some freshly baked bread, and a variety of cleaning aids. As the family ate, Mert, Dylan, and Clare swept and cleaned and polished and scrubbed. When they drove away, they left a sparkling clean house, a kettle of simmering stew, and a very grateful mother. On they went, to visit a restless boy who had been confined to his bed for a month; to take clothing to a family whose father had lost his job and had had to start over, working for less pay; to prepare a good meal for a couple who had just returned from a long, exhausting journey.

Dylan worked faster than he had known he could, racing against the shadows that steadily grew longer and longer as the sun traveled across the sky. He so longed to be back at the chapel before sunset, still hopeful that, perhaps, the Founder would come and he would meet him. Even in the middle of such tiring work, Dylan never stopped thinking about the Founder. He found himself, over and over, telling people about him. Even though he was just learning about the Founder himself, what he knew so far begged to be told, and tell it Dylan did. He told tired discouraged adults about how the Founder had called him out of the cave. He told families struggling to meet their own needs how, all along his journey, the Founder had been leaving him everything he needed. When Dylan gave aid to those whose need had resulted from their own poor choices, he freely told them how he had lost his pass in a fight and how the Founder had paid his fine. Everywhere he went, he realized that he knew something about the Founder that seemed helpful to the situation. *And I've never even met him,* Dylan thought to himself. *Oh, I hope we get back in time.*

Lunchtime came and went and the afternoon wore on. Still the three workers worked, washing dishes, weeding yards, cleaning toilets, cutting grass, heating meals. They visited sick and lonely people; they played with restless children; they delivered gifts and supplies. And all the while, Dylan tried not to notice how late it grew. Finally, they pulled up in front of the last house. This was the home where the refrigerator would be delivered, to an elderly lady whose old refrigerator had finally worn out and who had no money to buy another. Mert had a hand truck that helped him and Dylan a great deal in moving the refrigerator; however, the lady's house was small and full of her personal treasures, so maneuvering the large appliance through the house and around corners required a great deal of strategy and many starts and stops. They finally succeeded in installing the refrigerator, and in convincing the happy woman that they really must go now, and headed back to the empty truck. Mert jumped in the air, clicking his heels together playfully. "Wa-hoo!" he cried. "We did it! We're done!"

Immediately, Mert realized that, though Dylan smiled with genuine happiness for him, Dylan himself looked dejected. Mert stopped in his tracks. "Oh dear!" he said. "You wanted to be back at the chapel by sundown, didn't you?" And Mert glanced at the sun, just about to sink below the horizon.

Dylan shook his head. "That's okay," he said. "I still think we did the right thing. I just really would have liked to meet the Founder." He sighed. "Too late now, though; our passes have expired. Mert, there's a gate on the road that we came through, just past the overlook where you look down into Holiday. Could you drive us back there, please? It's time for us to go home."

"Sure, I can take you wherever you like," Mert said as they all climbed into the cab and he turned the truck's ignition. The truck rumbled off down the road. "Do you mean to tell me," Mert asked, "that you've never met the Founder?"

Dylan nodded unhappily.

"Hm," Mert replied. "I was sure you had met him."

"*You* haven't even met him," Dylan protested. "You said so yourself."

"I said no such thing!" Mert answered. "Of course I've met him. Why do you think I spend so much time at this job?"

"No," Dylan insisted, "*I* said I'd never met the Founder and *you* said, 'Neither have I.'"

"No," Mert corrected him, "you said you'd never *seen* the Founder and I said, 'Neither have I.'" Then he added, "Are you *sure* you've never met him?"

"I'm sure," Dylan answered with finality. "Do you think you could meet him and not know it?"

Mert considered. "It's not likely," he agreed. But then he added, almost under his breath, "But it has happened."

The truck rumbled on, its passengers riding in silence. It drove through the streets of Holiday, even more beautiful as lights began twinkling on in the gathering dusk—and as Dylan realized he would never come here again. Mert took a steep one-way route up the hill and approached the gate where "Proof of Life" had been required when Dylan and Clare had first entered, four days ago. As they drew near the gate and the truck slowed, Dylan realized a group of—was it people? Or animals?—stood by it. Mert pulled off to the side of the road and shut off the engine.

Dylan and Clare got out of the truck cab, staring at the figures in front of them. The candlemaker of Holiday Village was there, easily seen by the light of the bright candle he held. In his other hand, the candlemaker held a bell. It looked just like the choir director Dylan had talked with up in the steeple of the church on the hill. With chest puffed up proudly as usual, the penguin stood by the candlemaker, waiting. Near him, on a high stool, sat the man who had first told Dylan he needed to be authorized to get into Holiday. Although before, Dylan would have said that all trees look alike, he was sure that the tree just by the side of the road was *his* tree, the one that had spoken with him in the forest. Yes, and there stood the little tree right next to it. Dylan was half-conscious of a question in his mind—*how did they* get *here?*—but he was too busy looking around for other new acquaintances to puzzle over it now. Yes, down at the bottom of the tree was a poinsettia plant, speaking quietly to a bunch of mistletoe that held to the tree's trunk. Dylan could just make out the sound of the voice, without discerning any words. The voice sounded like that of his grandmother. Looking up, Dylan could see the very first stars of the evening. There were two. One star was obviously very close, for it shone very brightly. Next to it was a small twinkly one.

Feeling like he was in a dream, Dylan moved slowly toward the group gathered at the gate. Turning around to speak to Clare, who was just behind him, he shut his mouth without saying anything. Someone he had not seen before had just concluded a quick, quiet conversation with Mert and was moving forward too. Dylan stood still and waited for the man to catch up to them. The man wore clothes that were clean, but which were clearly intended for the out of doors. He had a tan, weathered face and carried what Dylan recognized as a shepherd's staff. Dylan's eyes quickly darted around, looking for some sheep, but he saw none.

The rugged man drew near to Dylan and smiled, his kindly eyes twinkling. "My friend Mert here says you want to find the Founder," he said.

Dylan nodded. "But I realize that you don't find the Founder, he finds you."

The shepherd smiled again, and nodded once. "That's right," he said. "And you don't think you've been found?"

Dylan opened his mouth to answer, then closed it again. He wasn't sure what the shepherd meant.

"There are all kinds of reasons to believe you *have* been found," the shepherd continued.

A voice spoke from the side of the road and Dylan turned to face the tree. (He had been right; it *was* "his" tree.) "I told you it was the Founder's voice you heard back in the cave," the tree said in a grave voice, to which, this time, the lighthearted little tree added nothing. "He called you out. If he hadn't, you would still be sitting there."

The gatekeeper stepped off his stool and chimed in. "Yes, and how do you think you found the flyer about Holiday in the first place? Didn't it look to you like it had been set there on purpose, leaning against the fence like that, just waiting for you to find it?"

It seemed to Dylan that his brain was functioning very slowly. "Did you put it there?" he asked.

The gate guard shook his head hard. "Nope, not me," he answered. "The Founder did. He *wanted* you to come looking for him."

Dylan looked down as Missy Mistletoe began to speak. "Who paid your fine, when you lost your pass?" she asked simply. "And who planned your way through that neighborhood where you saw so many things about yourself that you didn't like? Could it be that the Founder had found you?"

"Who sent me to bring light when you were lost in the darkness?" the candlemaker asked. "Why did *you* get out into the light while the Darkness Dwellers are still in there?"

From the candlemaker's hand, the bell spoke up. "Remember how you had plenty of really good things to eat and water to drink, even up on top of the mountain? How did it get there for you, if the Founder didn't bring it? Why would he give you what you needed if he hadn't found you?"

There was a pause, then, which Dylan found awkward at first, until he realized that it was the star's turn to talk, and everyone was waiting for her voice to reach them. Finally it came. She said, in her whispered roar of a voice, "We stars shine on everyone. Everyone sees us. Who hears what we say about the Founder—except those who have been found? You heard us, Dylan. You've been found."

"By the Founder!" said another smaller voice, full of excitement, also coming from high in the sky.

The penguin stepped forward. His chest puffed just a little more. "If you didn't know the Founder, you'd be just as productive as those dead, bare trees in the winter wasteland, back by my place."

"If you didn't know the Founder," Penny Poinsettia added, "you wouldn't want to give him a gift."

Mert stepped forward, eagerly. "But you do know the Founder. And you did give him a gift. You gave your last day in Holiday to helping other people, which is just what he would have wanted."

Now even Clare got into the act. "And Dylan, you yourself said you wanted to do that because you really thought it was what the Founder would want, that it's what he would have done himself. You *do* know the Founder, Dylan; you've even begun to think like he does."

Could it be true? Did the Founder know him? Had the Founder found him? Is that why he had been so obsessed with finding the Founder? "But I've never seen him," Dylan still objected.

"None of us have seen him either," the shepherd answered. "There were those who saw him once, but that was a long time ago. No one's seen him for a long time now. But we all know him, just the same. And love him. You may not have seen him, but he's been with you all along. You have a long ways to go in getting to know him. You'll need to work on that every day of your life. But you can stop worrying about finding him. You *have* found him, because he's found you."

The shepherd cleared his throat, stood up straight, and recited:

"You don't have to find the Founder; he's found you.
When the Founder finds you, he makes you a finder too."

Everyone responded with absolute silence. Then the shepherd winked. "It *rhymes!*" he announced, and the whole crowd, not least of all Dylan, exploded in laughter. Dylan laughed and laughed, until he could no longer breathe. He looked over at Clare who was holding her sides, doubled over. The gatekeeper was wiping tears of laughter from his face while even the candlemaker had set down his candle because he was shaking uncontrollably. The laughter went on, peal after peal, with no one in any hurry to stop.

When Dylan finally gained control of himself, he saw the shepherd smiling at him. "Look at your pass," he said. Dylan pulled the green visitor's pass from his pocket. Dylan had no idea how or when it had happened, but words had been stamped across his pass. He read, "Permanent authorization to keep Holiday all year, in all places, and at all times."

"Thank you, all of you," Dylan said. "And now I really must get home." He turned to Clare. "Let's go," he said. "We've got to get back to Mom and Dad. They're going to want to know about this."